THE RED GIRL
Interviews with a Monster Hunter
-First edition-

CW01502112

Author:
George Hâ

2020

ISBN: 9798558867435

Cover design by George Hâncu

"Let parents bequeath to their children not riches, but the spirit of reverence."

Plato

CHAPTER I

BARK BOY

-So, let's get right to it, mister Rotaru. I understand you call yourself a "monster hunter".

-Please, call me Victor. I didn't catch your name.

-My name is Madelyn Hamilton. I'll be interviewing you today.

-So, Madelyn, what did you do?

-Excuse me?

-What did you do to deserve this? You obviously don't want to be here.

-As an adult, I am used to not always getting my way.

-Are you? It doesn't seem like it.

-Well, Victor, I'm an investigative journalist. A damn good one. But I guess all it takes is a corruption story about a certain senator, friend of my boss, to get me... this.

-I see... I'm your punishment.

-Look, don't take this the wrong way, but this is not my thing. I'm interested in the big stuff, the gritty stuff, the stories that need to get told.

-So, you are a risk-taker. Good! This may work out well for both of us.

-No offense, Victor, but publishing a story about some monster hunter isn't a risk for someone like me. It's professional suicide.

-Perhaps that is what your boss intends.

-Let's just get this over with. At least you seem to be a normal, sane individual.

-What I seem to be and what I truly am are two different things.

-All right... Tell me about yourself. Where were you born?

-My name is Victor Rotaru, as you know. I was born in Romania in 1977, in the Transylvanian city of Alba Iulia. There was a great earthquake that year, and my mother went into labor during the mayhem. The earthquake didn't hit hard where we lived but I was born in the back seat of a car, because my mother never made it to the hospital... She died giving birth to me.

-That must have been awful.

-I don't remember any of it, obviously.

-So, your father raised you alone?

-My father couldn't raise me. I ended up living with my grandparents for the first seven years of my life. My grandfather was a mystic, always telling me fantastic stories. My grandmother was a kind but strong woman. One day, while we were returning from a vacation in the Apuseni Mountains, grandfather ran into a deer on the road and the vehicle then hit an oak tree. He and my grandmother died instantly.

-Again, awful... What did you do?

-It was already getting dark and the road was less traveled. I remember being cold and scared. The car was full of blood... I just ran out and never looked back.

-Just like that? Did someone find you?

-You could say that. I must have run half a mile down the road before I heard a voice, inside my head. It was a strange feeling. I couldn't tell if it was male or female. I can still hear it...

-What did the voice say?

-It told me to calm down. It told me to stop running.

-Did you?

-Not at first, but then I remembered what my grandfather said, about forest spirits. He said they speak to you without sound, in your time of need... If you are worthy, that is.

-What happened next?

-I eventually stopped running. The voice told me to walk to the tree line, at the side of the road. What followed changed my life forever.

-Go on, then.

-I saw a massive dark figure, just beyond the first trees. It told me to follow.

-This is like one of those comic book origin stories my nephew keeps obsessing about.

-I'm not familiar with those but yes, in a way it is how I came to be who I am today. That's why I need you to understand... I see you smiling. Should I go on?

-Don't be offended if I'm a bit skeptical, but go on.

-As I said, I started following the dark figure who led me deep into the woods. Eventually, we reached a small pond covered with dead leaves, by the side of a cliff. The figure told me that I needed to speak to its master. Suddenly, the pond started whispering and the dead leafs all disappeared. I heard another voice, more powerful and commanding than the first. The voice belonged to someone who called himself the Messenger.

-So, basically, you were just hearing voices?

-It's hard to describe. Before you question my sanity, you need to hear the whole story. The Messenger told me that I walked the realm between the world of the living and that of the dead. He told me that I needed to make a choice. If there was nothing else I desired from life, all I needed to do was to walk off the side of the cliff, and he would send me away to the realms beyond. However, if I wanted to return amongst the living, he could help me.

-That seems like a very scary choice for a seven-year-old, one who just saw his grandparents get killed.

-It was and still is the hardest choice I had to make.

-You obviously chose to stick around. What made you do that?

-The Messenger told me that if I choose to return, I will forever be bound to the Realm of the Undecided. I would see and hear things that others couldn't. This would make my life even more difficult. If I returned, I needed a purpose and I needed guidance. That is why he offered me a deal.

-Let me guess: Serve his sinister goals and you will get eternal life?

-Not at all. My life was my own and believe me, I am mortal. The Messenger told me that the entities from the Realm of the Undecided would mostly stay hidden from me and those like me.

-Those like you?

-The Touched. Those very few who have walked through the gates of death and returned amongst the living.

-So what was the deal?

-It was more of an oath, on my part. Since I would gain superhuman senses, I needed to understand how to use them. The Messenger told me that there are three types of entities roaming the Realm of the Undecided. The first where the Angry Ones. They are driven by rage and the desire for vengeance against the living. They are what we would call "bad spirits".

-Like ghosts, right? The dangerous kind?

-Like ghosts, but not the dangerous kind. The Angry Ones are very common actually. More common than you think. They are usually harmless, as far as humanity is concerned. They are easy to understand and control. Their conflicts get resolved or forgotten, and their hatred can quickly turn to compassion.

- So, which are the dangerous spirits?

- The second kind of entity in the Realm of the Undecided is the Guardian. They are those who have unfinished business, like the Angry Ones, but exist solely with the desire to protect someone or something. As you can imagine, they are what you would call "guardian angels". They often get into conflict with the Angry Ones and their energies cancel each other out.

-So that's why the bad spirits aren't so dangerous.

-That's part of it, yes. This war has been going on since the creation of the Universe. It's more like a dance really, between light and darkness.

-You know, my grandmother always said she had a guardian angel who saved her multiple times. I never paid much attention to that... Anyway, so far so good.

-The third type of entity is called the Lost. They are extremely rare. Not more than a dozen each generation become lost. They are neither good nor bad, as far as our basic definitions go. They are extremely dangerous though.

-So being dangerous is not bad?

-Danger itself is bad, as far as we are concerned, yes. But the Lost are almost never responsible for any harm caused. They do not intend to inflict themselves upon us, one way or another. They are in fact void of any purpose.

-Hence the name.

-Indeed. However, the Lost have a unique ability to attract elder entities. You see, being void of all will makes you a vessel begging to become full. It makes you a beacon to all those who wish to interact with us humans, while breaking all the rules.

-So they become possessed?

-They become abominations, twisted experiments of unnatural origin and unclear purpose. They are game-breakers, as I call them.

-You mean to suggest that they ignore the rules of nature?

-Yes! Life, nature, and everything that has an order to it.

-That's interesting... So, the truly dangerous ones are those who start out aimless. An empty mind is a dangerous thing, right?

-You could say that.

- I'm guessing they are your so-called "monsters".

-Obviously. The Lost are the only true monsters I know. All the others are just misunderstood creatures, as it turns out.

-Ok, I admit your story seems interesting... And you don't appear to be a madman.

-The story is just beginning.

-But what made you want to tell it? Why now?

-That is a revelation for a later time. For now, let's get back to the scared young boy, in the middle of a dark forest.

-All right.

-As I said, that night changed my life forever. The oath I made to the Messenger was to always keep my eyes open and do whatever I could to stop the corruption of the Lost from spreading to our world.

-So, that night you agreed to become a monster hunter.

-I prefer to call myself a banisher. I contact the Lost and help them achieve... order.

-You mean kill them.

-It is only the shell that dies when the elder entity is separated from it. But none of us truly die.

-Sounds like you almost did, that night.

-You see, that night I almost became lost myself. The dark entity rescued me and delivered me to the Messenger. Instead of becoming an abomination, a vessel of chaos, I was given a choice: Pass on, or fight those who weren't as lucky as I was.

-What happened next? How did you get out of there?

-After taking my oath, the Messenger said he would speak to me again. Moments later, I woke up in the back seat of my grandfather's car, with a massive headache and a couple of broken ribs. Some villagers from a nearby farm were approaching, having heard the crash. I saw them running down the road and my first instinct was to hide. I didn't want to go back to live with my father. I didn't want to be a burden, you see. That was my judgment at the time... I left the car and ran crouched to some nearby bushes, where I stayed hidden as the villages inspected the vehicle and eventually called the police. I knew there would be some hours before anyone realized I was missing. I planned to use that time to scout the area and find a place to sleep, hidden away. In my naiveté, I decided I would be a forest dweller, living off the land and making friends with all the beasts and spirits.

-Poor kid… You must have felt so alone.

-I did. I felt like I had to make my own way, from then on. Strangely, I don't remember being scared.

-How did you survive? I suppose you were discovered at some point.

-Years later.

-Years? Do you mean to tell me that you survived all alone in the woods, for several years? That's just crazy!

-I did… The first nights were the hardest. I found an abandoned shack that was once used by gypsy loggers. It had a single window, no glass, and it smelled like piss and rot.

-So you just… lived there?

-There was a stream close by. I cleaned the shack and repaired the bed… I went without food for several nights before I found some berry bushes. Later, I started stealing chickens and vegetables from the nearby village.

-Didn't the police look for you?

-They probably did, for a while. But I suppose a missing kid wasn't that big of a deal to a failing communist regime.

-Didn't the villagers see you around?

-Some of them did, but I always traveled at night, at the edge of the village, covered in leaves and tree bark for camouflage.

-That was clever of you.

-I suppose it was… Years later I heard there was a whole legend regarding my appearances. The villagers called me ''bark boy''. They would warn their children not to stay out late, or I would find them and eat them. Ha-ha!

-Ha-ha! Bark Boy! I like that. I suppose you must have run into some kids messing around, during all that time.

- I did, but that's not important. During those two and a half years things happened, things that changed me. I learned to think like a wild beast while remaining essentially human. I talked to spirits... More importantly, later that summer I would come face to face with my first monster...

-Ok, I guess we'll talk about that next time.

-Yes, next time.

CHAPTER 2

THE RED GIRL

-So, Victor, we're getting to the interesting stuff now.

-Don't tell me that you have decided to believe me, since last week.

-I decided to give you the benefit of a doubt. If there's one thing you learn as a journalist, it's that no one knows everything.

-Fair enough.

-Last time you were going to tell me about your first monster encounter.

-I was, yes. I call her... the Red Girl.

-Call her? Didn't you kill her or banish her or whatever?

-I did not. I thought I did, at the time. But I was young and had no experience with such abominations.

-Tell me what happened.

-One summer morning, while I was gathering berries in the woods, I spotted a rabbit and ran after it with my makeshift spear. I had just stolen a knife from the village and had started carving some basic tools. Soon after, I approached a small clearing and the rabbit disappeared into the tall grass... In the middle of the clearing, I saw a girl. She must have been a few years older than me.

-So around 10 years old?

-Sounds about right.

-She held the rabbit in her hands and fed it from her palm.

-What did she look like?

-She had this amazing red hair, which shined like a blazing fire in the morning light. She was... beautiful.

-Was she one of the village girls?

-I thought so, for a few moments. But then I noticed her skin shined as if it glittered with precious stones, and she didn't make a single sound while stepping on the grass.

-She sounds like an angel or something.

-She was, as far as I was concerned. In fact, that is the first thing I asked her.

-What did she say?

-She smiled and made a gesture with her finger, indicating that she wasn't.

-Didn't she talk?

-She didn't say a single word but she didn't need to. I was a kid, all alone in the woods. She took my hand and led me to the middle of the clearing. There we sat down and I saw rabbits, lizards, and even a deer get close to us. It's like we weren't even there.

-Didn't the animals see you?

-They saw us, but were unafraid. Her presence drew them to us, like a magnet.

-Well, it doesn't sound to me like she was a monster.

-She even had a calming effect on me. I felt at peace, for the first time in months. We just sat there for hours, petting rabbits and enjoying the warm sunlight... But then, it started to get dark. As soon as the sun dropped low and the sky took a reddish color, I noticed a change. The animals would no longer approach us. Also, the glow disappeared from the girl's skin and moved to her eyes. The darker it got, the more they shined. I felt my heart beating faster and faster. The wonder was gone and was quickly replaced by a quiet... despair.

-She turned into something else, didn't she?

-The transformation was ever so gradual, and was more a change of heart, on my part. The girl was still beautiful. Her smile somehow got... wider. But her beauty was no longer fascinating to me. It was... unsettling, unnatural.

-Did you run away?

-Her grip on my arm got tighter as her hands became colder than death. I knew that soon I would not have the strength to overpower her and break free. I had to act... I got up slowly and told her that I needed to go. I told her that my parents were waiting for me back home. I lied and could immediately tell that she knew it. She made the same gesture with her finger, as before. But then, something strange happened: She just let go of my arm and pointed in the direction of my hut.

-She knew where you lived... Damn!

-I got the feeling that she knew everything. There was no point in lying or hiding from her. Her eyes could pierce into one's soul... I slowly backed up and watched her stand there, in the same spot, without making a move. Suddenly, as I was approaching the tree line, she started walking towards me as if she had changed her mind. She started sprinting. I turned around and started running myself. As I reached the trees, I tripped on a root and fell to the ground. Naturally, I was convinced that my clumsiness would be the end of me, but, as I once again turned around, I saw her just standing there, at the edge of the clearing. At my side, I saw the same dark figure that had led me to the Messenger, weeks before.

-She was afraid of it?

-No, I don't think she was afraid of anything... The figure spoke to me: "Behold, an abomination!" it said, in a sober and chilling voice. I asked what it was and the figure explained that the Red Girl had once been a village girl who had gotten lost into the woods. Her parents had beaten her because she hadn't done her chores. She didn't hate them, but, much like me, she didn't want to be around them anymore... She went to that clearing and just sat there, barefoot, crying for days. The animals approached her, sensing her innocence. But she was starving and before long grabbed a rabbit and twisted its neck. She had seen her dad do the same, to chickens. She ate it raw... She died after a few weeks of suffering, there, in that same clearing. The tall grass covered her and hid her body from view. Badgers and wolves fed on her body until there was nothing left.

-The innocence was gone.

-Her soul wandered that clearing aimlessly, until a powerful entity called Urrud the Corruptor found her. He turned her into an abomination the sole purpose of which was corrupting and twisting everything pure and true... Or so it appeared.

-The figure didn't know the whole story.

-Indeed. He couldn't know. Urrud was a mystery from beyond this Universe.

-So, the Red Girl was stuck there, in that clearing?

-Yes, her possessed shell could not leave during the night, as her corruption was rejected by the forest. During the day, Urrud would leave and allow her to roam freely, appearing to children in the surrounding villages. She would lure them to that clearing and... twist them.

-She didn't kill them?

-Se only killed animals for energy, at night. I went there night after night, observing her. Most of the time she cried with a sinister and terrible yell, as her bloodied teeth ripped into the flesh of small animals.

- Ok, I get it. She was terrifying. But what made her more dangerous than your average ghost?

- Because through her, Urrud's unnatural influence would leak into our world, and everyone she touched would spread the corruption further, for years to come.

-Even you?

-I... was not a normal kid. I would have resisted her attempts better but yes, in the end, even I would have become tainted.

-How did you kill her?

-I didn't.

-Oh, that's right. I forgot!

-After observing her for a while, I determined that she couldn't touch me if I wore my tree bark suit. Something about the structure of trees... repelled her. One night, I entered the clearing wearing my camouflage and chased all the animals away, just to see what she would do.

-You attempted to starve her?

-Something like that. Needless to say, she wasn't very happy about that. She started screaming at me so loudly and terribly that it literally chilled me to the bone... But I didn't stop. I went there night after night and took her food away. After about a week, when I got to the clearing she wasn't moving around as usual. I got the sense that she was weekend, so I approached her, cautiously. Then, I heard it.

-Heard what?

-The most terrible and menacing voice I had ever heard in my life. I immediately realized it was the demon Urrud speaking, not the girl.

-What did he say?

-He asked me what I wanted. I told him that I would kill the Red Girl and free her trapped soul... Urrud laughed. He told me to go ahead. He... even promised that if I succeeded, he would abandon his attempts to corrupt humanity.

-That sounds like a good deal... Too good, right?

-Urrud is many things, but he is not a deceiver or a common liar.

-Really? And how did you know that?

-I did not know it at the time, but I was just a kid. I simply believed his words were genuine. As it turns out, they were... However, that's a story for another time.

-Wait, this doesn't make any sense. How can a demon and corruptor not be a deceiver?

-I don't have all the answers, Miss Hamilton. I do know that even demons have rules they abide by. Perhaps he was just amused by my ignorance and desired to play games.

-Why do I get the distinct feeling that there's something you're not telling me?

-These interviews have a purpose. I wish to convey a message. Have patience, Miss Hamilton.

-All right. Go on.

-After my encounter with Urrud, I continued starving the Red Girl, night after night. As she grew more and more hungry, her screams got louder. I wondered if the villagers could hear her, or if I was the only one who witnessed her suffering... After a few more nights, her desperation caused her to attack me, even with my tree armor on. She pushed me so hard that pieces of bark flew off and one of my shoulders became exposed. She went into a frenzy and immediately jumped on me, trying to bite the vulnerable area. I hit her over the head with a large stick and ran away. As I observed her form the edge of the forest, I noticed her hands and head were bleeding. The blood was black and quickly evaporated into a dark mist, as soon as it touched the ground. At that moment, I knew she could be killed... The next morning, I went into the clearing looking for her, to see what my efforts had amounted to. I waited for hours until the Red Girl finally returned. She was no longer smiling, but her hands and head were untouched. It was as if nothing had happened. She reached for my hand, like the first time, but I didn't allow her to touch me. This made her sad. She turned away from me ad ran out of the clearing. I felt guilty, as if I was torturing the poor girl.

-Perhaps that's what the demon wanted, to use your humanity against you... Ha! Some of my colleagues do that sometimes.

-Regardless, I remained determined to stay the course. A few days later, I saw her dancing in the clearing with another little girl, a girl from the village. I tried to intervene, to save the little girl, but when they saw me, they both ran off towards the village, where she knew I wouldn't follow.

-What happened to the other girl?

-I never saw her again, but I think the Red Girl met with her regularly, as she probably did with other children. That night she seemed to have renewed strength. It appeared that bringing children to her place of feeding gave her renewed energy. I understood that starving her would be more difficult than I thought. I now spent a good part of my day trying to scare children away from the woods, but it was pointless. The Red Girl knew that eventually, just like her, I had to eat. That meant leaving her unattended for hours, while I foraged or sneaked into the village. She soon learned to match her feeding patterns to mine. So, as you say, my humanity was my weakness.

-Yeah, but not the emotional part. Anyway, how did the story end?

-Frustrated by my inability to starve my possessed antagonist, I decided to fight her, to the death. Armed with a bunch of sharp sticks and a makeshift club, I entered the clearing one night, when she was weaker than usual, thanks to my partially successful tactics. It was make or break time... and I knew it. I remember every detail of that night. I had just eaten a piece of cornbread, so I felt strong. I charged her with everything I had, stabbing her repeatedly with the sticks. Her dark blood turned to mist and filled the air with a rotten smell. Her terrible screams pierced the night. Eventually, she fell to the ground. I grabbed my club and started hitting her ferociously over the head. I felt like a wild beast... I felt strong.

-Did you enjoy it, hitting her?

-You must remember, Miss Hamilton, the Red Girl was no longer human... But I must mention that when she finally stopped moving, my euphoria quickly faded and a great sadness filled my heart. I was just a kid, who felt like he had just beaten another kid to death, after starving her.

-Seems like Urrud succeeded.

-Yes, he managed to take away my innocence... What was left of it, anyway. I heard Urrud's laughter, as he congratulated me. I felt weak, drained of all my energy.

-You had quite a fight.

-It wasn't the fight that made me so weak. It was the hatred spent, feeding Urrud's corruption.

-So, by killing her, you made him stronger.

-I thought that I had killed her, but I was wrong. My drained energy flowed like a river towards the Red Girl's body, reviving her. She rose, and I saw her eyes glow stronger than ever, flooding the misty air with a yellow light. I quickly escaped the kill zone, before she could grab me... I heard Urrud's voice again. He congratulated me on my effort and reminded me that his promise still stood: If I managed to kill the Red Girl, he would leave our world for good. As he finished saying those words, the lost girl vanished before my eyes, in a cloud of dark mist...

-Did you ever see her again?

-You have no patience, Miss Hamilton. You just want to know how the story ends.

-And you want to keep me hooked, so that you can get your message across, whatever that is.

-There's a reason why things follow a natural course, in life. Don't attempt to break that order, Miss Hamilton.

-I'll... try. Go on, please.

-The Red Girl became an obsession of mine. Years later, when I finally left the woods, I started looking for signs of her corruption everywhere. I never forgot Urrud's words and the terrifying might of his voice... I made it my mission to stop him. As it turned out, that was more difficult than I could ever have imagined. But...

-Let me guess, that's a story for next week.

-That is a story for many weeks, my dear.

CHAPTER 3

THE ARMY OF SHADOWS

-Welcome back, Miss Hamilton.

-I think it's time you called me Madelyn.

-All right, Madelyn.

-So, good news: My pig of a boss finally let me off the hook. I can go back to writing political articles.

-That is good news, for you.

-Oh, don't worry, I have decided to keep our appointments, regardless. Your story is intriguing. It would make quite the novel. That's my suggestion, in fact. I think your messages would be better received in that format, rather than being compressed in a simple article. The volume of information is just too high, and skipping out on all the details would just ruin it all. What do you think?

- I don't know. I never thought about it like that. I just have a message to communicate. Professional defect, I guess. Always keep the goal clear in mind.

-I think your goal would be better served this way. I'll just record and write down everything you say, and when we're all done I'll even talk to a literary agent, a good friend of mine. She knows all the major New York publishers.

-Hmmm, I'll have to think about that. In the meantime, let's continue with the story... Shall we?

-Of course. I'm curious to know how you made it out of the woods.

-Well, it wasn't easy and I didn't even want to do it, at first. After two years though, it became apparent that I couldn't keep it up. I was severely malnourished, I had no new clothes, and, worst of all, I felt my humanity slipping away. I feared I would become mad, which is not something a nine-year-old boy should be worried about.

-The winters must have been the worst.

-Yes and no. My body suffered from the cold and getting food was a lot harder but, at the same time, my mind was at rest. You see, I would just build a fire in my shack's rusty iron stove and lay in bed all day, learning to read with some old books I had stolen. No monsters and no spirits bothered me in there.

By the second winter, I was quite the reader. The village school had to replace half of its books after New Year, since I broke into their library.

-It still amazes me that no one found you out there.

-I was very careful and I developed quite the sense of hearing. I could hear people coming half a mile away, even on windy days.

-So it's true that in isolation some of your senses become heightened?

-Just those you use extensively, in my experience. The ones your life depends on. It's amazing how nature gives you a helping hand when you need it most. I also developed my special senses, during this time. I was even able to communicate with some of the entities from beyond our world.

-Did you ever meet another monster, out there?

-I don't think I did. Just some Angry Ones. They learned to steer clear of me, after a while. I didn't bother them and they didn't bother me.

-So, how did you eventually leave the shack?

-As the third winter came along, things got bad. I was starving. Alerted by all my nigh-time activities, the villagers took precautions. Finding food vas more and more difficult. I was eventually forced to scout further and further, to

22

neighboring villages. One night, while I was on one of my usual runs to a faraway village, I just dropped from exhaustion into someone's barn. I slept in there with the pig. The smell was bad but it was better than freezing to death.

-I can't even imagine how that's like.

-I was used to hardship. I never complained or pitied myself. I just kept breathing, like a stray dog. Anyway, the next morning, as I left the barn, a little girl found me and asked me my name. As we were talking, her father came along and saw me, frozen half to death and skinny as an old scarecrow. He didn't recognize me from the village kids, so he immediately took an interest. As it turns out, he was the village priest.

-I guess you got lucky. Did he take you in?

-He took me to the kitchen, put some good shoes on me, and fed me some hot soup. He realized I was homeless. They were poor, but not even the poor kids had shoes that looked as bad as mine. I had to cut them because they wouldn't fit me, after two years.

-Did he report you to the police?

-Not at first. He and his wife argued about it for days, but they decided I needed to go to school. They saw a spark in me, I guess. I told them some bullshit story about my parents abandoning me years ago and gave them the name Victor.

-Hold on, so your real name isn't Victor?

- I was born Constantin Domnaru. I took the name Victor Rotaru when the priest and his wife adopted me. Normally, I would have gone to an orphanage but the priest had connections with the local police and child services. He worked a miracle, I guess.

-Not a godly one, but still impressive.

-Miracles only come from one place, Madelyn. Anyway, after I got settled in, I started school but I also helped with the work in the field. I had quite the unusual energy, once I got some proper food in me. It didn't take the priest long to realize there was something odd about me. I would leave at night for long walks without telling anyone and I would talk to myself on occasion. I also had great resistance to the cold. My step sister Mary would get sick often but I could walk barefoot in the snow without any repercussions. My toughness was handy when it came to working, so the priest didn't complain, at first.

-I'm guessing things changed. Priests aren't known for their tolerance towards ghost whisperers.

- Some of them are, but not Ioan. He tolerated me for years, and I couldn't blame him for anything. I had a roof over my head and a full stomach. I felt normal, for a change.

-Why didn't you try to find your real father?

-I felt useful in the priest's house. I earned my keep. Back home I would just have been a burden, since my father was a widower and a busy engineer. That was the reason I ran away in the first place, as I told you.

-So you'd rather risk your own life and work in the fields at age 10 than having to rely on someone else?

-It's not just about the trust issues, though I prefer to keep things...transactional with most humans. I also prefer my independence, my freedom. That was the best part of living in the woods all that time. I learned to rely on myself and make my own way.

-I get it... What about your secret life? Did you have any encounters while living with the priest and his family?

-Not for many years. I mean, I did spot the occasional harmless spirit but I had grown numb to that. As I said, I almost felt normal... Of course, all of that changed when I met an old woman one night, in front of the church. I must have been 11 or 12 at the time. At first, she seemed normal, but as I approached her I could tell something was wrong.

She had long bony fingers, white as a sheet. There was a funeral that day and she was the one they buried. Her spirit decided to stick around for a while, as they often do. The strange thing is, when she saw me, she immediately realized who… what I was. It's like she was waiting for me. She backed up as if she was scared, as if I scared her.

-She saw something in you.

-Yes, she saw the darkness within. She told me that she had a message for me, from a demon that had plagued her family for generations. She was shaking and was obviously suffering. She told me that the demon would not release her until I have heard her words.

-So, what was the message?

-She said that The Army of Shadows was coming and that I needed to prepare. She said I would have to fight them, in order to save my soul, and the souls of my children, if I ever had any. Naturally, I asked her why. Why was this army of monsters coming for me? Her answer shook me to my core. Her skin got dark and she grew tall, as tall as the church. Her eyes were glowing with a familiar glow of evil. I only saw that glow once before, in the Red Girl's eyes.

-And the answer?

-The abomination in front of me now spoke with a voice that I hoped I would never hear again. It was the voice of Urrud: "Did you really think you would be free of me, boy?" he said, laughing. He then reminded me of the promise he made me years before, in the clearing. He now wanted to turn that promise into a bargain, to drag me further into his twisted game. He said the old woman he had imprisoned had three sons and they had children of their own. The entire family was cursed and would remain cursed for nine more generations if I didn't play his game. He told me that I had the chance to be a hero, to set them free. All I had to do is hunt down and destroy the Red Girl, before his army of abominations would eventually kill me.

-He didn't give you much of a choice, did he?

-I could have refused him, but I would still be hunted. This way I had a chance to do some good, before the end. Or so I thought. I accepted and as soon as I said the words, the abomination shrank down and turned into the scared old woman once again. She thanked me with all her heart and begged me to free her granddaughter, Ileana, and end this terrible curse.

-I get it now. It was her granddaughter Ileana! She was the Red Girl.

-Indeed she was. The old woman had lost her years before. Many children from her family went missing. She lived her whole life carrying that burden, that soul-crushing weight no parent should endure.

-So even though you would not rely on others, you went out of your way to help them.

-It's what hurts the most, in my book.

-What does?

-Having to rely on others to save you. The feeling of helplessness is devastating. I understood that, but I also understood how much strength it takes to ask for help, sometimes.

- It's safe to say that your childhood forged you into a true hero, albeit an unconventional one.

-I never saw myself as a hero, Madelyn. I'm just a creature filled with purpose, much like you and your gritty journalism.

-But that's a good thing, right? Knowing your purpose.

-Only if it's your true purpose. And very few people learn theirs over the course of a single lifetime.

-You're speaking in riddles again.

-I have my reasons for not saying things outright.

-Yes, yes, I know. Have patience! So, this "Army of Shadows", what was it?

-I had yet to learn that but it was to become the reason why I would face more monsters in my lifetime than perhaps any other Touched. It would become the reason why I truly am a monster hunter.

-Let me guess, that's a story for another time.

-Precisely.

CHAPTER 4

THE SALAMANDER

-Good to see you, Madelyn.

-And you too, Victor.

-Busy week?

-Yes, why do you ask?

-You seem a little...unsettled. Did you get in trouble again?

-I always get in trouble, Victor. That's what happens when you have principles, in a world of chaos. Sometimes I wonder why I even bother.

-You are still young. One day you will realize you are not here to fight the world, or chaos itself.

-I thought that's what you did too.

-Oh no, I follow a path that keeps winding and turning. Every now and then, a hard choice comes along. That choice may set me on a different path, but it's still my own path.

- I don't get it.

- You see, it may appear as if life is all about choices, difficult choices and easy choices. Easy choices tell you nothing about yourself, about your nature. The hard choices, however, have a way of showing you who you truly are, what you stand for. How much control you have over those choices, is another matter.

-With you, so far. But don't these hard choices imply fighting to change things? To build a better world, to change our destiny?

-Every choice you make changes your world, Madelyn, fighting or no fighting. That should be enough. As for making the world a better place, I don't even know what that means. I know my better world differs from your better world. If so, doesn't fighting for a "better world" really mean fighting each other?

-You have a point, and I think the 20'Th century proved that quite well.

-Ah, yes, all those "better worlds" colliding with each other meant a century of murder and suffering. The echoes of it are still here: Idealism, ambition, dogmatism, and a fanatical belief in "a better world", your better world, only leads to more conflict.

-I've heard that before, but I can't just... stop. It's who I am.

-It's who you are right now. I'll tell you a secret Madelyn: All that conflict is just you fighting yourself. It's your own inner demons.

- And I have plenty of those, believe me.

-Oh, I'm beginning to see that.

-So is there no redemption for us, no hope?

-Not in this life, my dear. We are just here to learn, to catch a glimpse of the bigger picture, to place down a small piece of an endless puzzle.

-So, you do believe in absolute truth, something bigger than us.

-I do, but unlike most of us, I have seen things that convinced me of it.

-Yes, I suppose you have. Is your piece of the puzzle placed, then?

-I believe it's about to be placed, with your help, Madelyn.

-All right then, maybe it's time to get back to your story.

-So it is. Where were we?

-Let's see... You were telling me about the deal you made with Urrud and the Army of Shadows.

-The deal that changed my life... A hard choice. I was still a kid, no older than 12, but I knew that my choice to help others was somehow a choice to help myself.

-To better yourself?

- To find my own way. Life had led me to these choices, and I was about to confront things head-on.

-That's quite brave, for a kid.

-Cowering was never an option for me. Backing down meant death, most of the time. I learned early on to confront my demons.

-In your case, that sentence takes a whole new meaning. What did you do next?

-Nothing. I just kept living my life and going to school. I even made a few friends amongst the village kids. They thought I was weird but that fascinated them, somehow. I was as close to being happy as I ever was. But I knew it wouldn't last. I felt it.

-What happened next?

- It was early October, that same year, when strange things started happening in the fields around the village. The late harvests of vegetables and pumpkins were being destroyed, and no one knew why. Some sheep were disappearing as well.

At first people thought it was thieves and vandals but soon things took a turn for the sinister. Claw marks were found on pumpkins and strange lizard-like tracks were found in the mud alongside the secluded roads. People were getting scared, thinking it was some kind of unknown wild beast. Things only got worse in the next days. Strange purple lights were seen in the fields and in the marsh nearby, at night.

-I'm guessing you realized it was no ordinary beast.

-I was the only kid who dared going out at night, against my adoptive father's wishes, of course. One night I went to investigate the lights at the marsh behind the fields, when I saw a strange figure running through the rarefied October foliage. It ran on four legs but occasionally stopped and raised itself on the hind legs, supporting itself on a large tail.

-How big was it?

-It was taller than a man, when standing up, and a lot more massive. It had the stink of Urrud's corruption all over it. So, naturally, I went closer to investigate.

-Naturally.

-I had my trusty knife with me, but I knew it would probably not save me, in case of a direct confrontation. Still, it gave me some courage to step closer and watch it from the bushes. After a short time, the creature approached the marsh and went underwater. The water was glowing with a strange purple hue. I waited but it did not come out for the rest of the night. I think it may have sensed my presence.

-It was being cautious. A sign of intelligence.

-The next night I prepared myself. Before sunset, I climbed a large willow tree on the side of the pond. I took some rope and a small hatchet. I waited for hours before it finally showed up. The water started glowing and it came out of the pond, slowly. It immediately raised itself on two legs and started sniffing the air, mouth open. I could see its huge tongue, like a serpent's. It looked like a salamander only it was completely black, like a shadow almost. I baptized it the Shadow Salamander.

-Catchy. So, it was part of Urrud's army, I take it.

-Yes. I sensed it was looking for something or someone.

-You.

-We were hunting each other, playing a dangerous game of hide and seek.

-How could you even hope to defeat that thing? You were just a kid.

-It looked like it would take four strong men to overpower it, if they could somehow evade its sharp claws. I decided to use my cunning instead. I wanted to trap it. The next morning was a Sunday, so I skipped church, took a shovel and went to the marshes early. I started digging a hole next to the pond and filling it with sharp wooden spikes. Took me the whole day. It was only maybe a meter deep and started filling with water. Still, it was the best I could do. I covered it with sticks and placed some pumpkins around it. The cherry on top was a small mutton chop I managed to steal. I placed it on a bed of leaves, above the hole. The sun was already going down and I was tired. Still, I managed to climb the willow and waited patiently. My hands were bleeding from all the work. As soon as the sun went down, the pond started glowing and the Salamander appeared. It went straight for my trap and started tossing the pumpkins around. It jumped in and swallowed the mutton in one bite. Then, it suddenly stopped and started sniffing the air, quietly.

-Wait, so the stakes did nothing to it?

-My trap was a total failure. The fall was too short and the Salamander's skin was wet, slippery, and as tough as hardened leather. It didn't even flinch. I got scared and thought about running, but it was too late. It had caught the scent of my blood. It was a lesson learned the hard way. Abominations are drawn to human blood like moths to a flame.

-So what happened?

-In mere seconds it was climbing the tree, and looking me straight in the eyes. I thought I was going to die. I held out my knife, in front of my head, ready to strike, but I couldn't. I was paralyzed.

-Fear?

-Not only fear, Madelyn. The Salamander's gaze had a hypnotic effect on me. It prevented me from escaping. This was no dumb beast, but a skilled hunter.

-That must have been awful. You said you don't like feeling helpless.

-It started smelling me, its dark slimy tongue flipping through the cold air. Then, it spoke: "You are Victor", it said without words. I nodded my head, since I could not speak. "What are you doing here, Victor? Are you not afraid?" it uttered, almost kindly. I suddenly felt my vocal cords being released from the Salamander's grasp, as its sharp claws were dancing through the air, in a sinister choreography. I told it that I was not afraid. I lied. It started laughing and told me it was hungry. It was tired of raiding the fields for crops and livestock. When I asked it what it wanted to eat, it said: "your blood smells good. I will eat you, little one". I remember it as if it was yesterday. I was scared and I tried pleading for my life, saying I have a mission to fulfill. The monster was amused by my ramblings and finally said: "I will spare you, little one, but you must bring me another to take your place, before sunrise."

-Another deal...

-Another hard choice. No matter how tough I was, I still could not stop myself from shaking. I saw the Salamander become restless and I realized I had mere seconds to decide. I knew I could not lie to it, since it was obvious that it saw right through me. I could either sacrifice myself or doom another soul to be devoured alive.

-I pray to God I never have to make a choice like that.

-Like I said, Madelyn, choices like that teach us more about ourselves than years of reflection.

-So, you chose to sacrifice another. You chose to play God and decided who should die.

-I knew that fighting for my life was not an option. I would have been ripped apart in mere seconds. I promised the monster that I would bring another human to it, before sunrise. I hoped I would come up with a plan, fast. As I slowly walked back to the village, a million thoughts ran through my mind. Who should I choose? Who deserves to die? Does anyone deserve to be eaten alive? All terrible questions. I suppose I could have broken my promise and not bring another in my place, but I had a feeling the Salamander would not stop terrorizing the village until it tasted human flesh. I needed to act. Sunrise was only a few hours away and everyone was in their beds, sleeping, unaware of the grim reaper that was lurking in the shadows.

-You?

-Yes, I suddenly saw myself as a herald of death, as a servant to a dark master. The shame was unbearable. I could never kill anyone myself or convince an adult to follow me to the marsh, in the dead of night. A shadow was growing in my mind, an unthinkable notion that threatened my very humanity: I would have to take a child to the monster. I suppose that is what Urrud had intended, to further my corruption.

-Please don't tell me you actually did it, Victor.

-I went home and took my little sister Maria from her bed. I told her we were playing a game and she needed to be very quiet.

-I can't bear to hear this, Victor.

-I had a desperate plan, you see. As we approached the pond, I saw the dark figure crawling through the cold mud, boiling with anticipation. Maria was scared but never uttered a single word. She trusted me. To this day I do not understand why, but she had faith in me, perhaps more than I ever did. I gave Maria the sharpest knife we had in our kitchen. It was a knife

34

the priest's wife used to butcher meat, every Christmas. It had a long and sturdy blade. I told Maria that we were hunters and we must save the village from the beast. I told her that we must be brave for our parents and friends. She nodded and held the knife as tight as she could. As we approached, the Salamander was visibly excited: "You kept your promise, little one. But what's this you brought me? She's too small. I will have to eat both of you to sate my appetite!". Maria couldn't hear it. Only I had the gift.

-That was probably for the best.

-I believe so. Hearing that monster speak would have frightened her even more. The Salamander started crawling towards me, mouth open. It figured it should devour the strongest one of us first, because it would have been easy to catch a little girl running through the fields. I held my knife behind my back, waiting to strike. As the Salamander was ready to pounce and grab me, I gave Maria a sign. She jumped at the beast holding the long knife with both her little hands, and stabbed it in the right leg, right above the knee. It let out a terrible scream as it turned towards the now helpless Maria. It was my time to strike. I plunged the knife deep in the monster's muscular shoulder with all my strength. Visibly surprised and shocked, the beast span around and knocked us both off our feet with its tail. I managed to hold on to my knife while Maria left hers in the Salamander's leg. As it was trying to pull it out with its clumsy claws, I knew we had precious seconds to run. We couldn't get all the way to the village and we couldn't hide. I made a gamble and went for the willow tree again. I grabbed Maria by the hand and quickly pushed her up to the highest branches. Below us, the Salamander was crawling towards the tree, having removed the knife. A purple glowing blood was dripping out of its leg and shoulder. The abomination was badly wounded but it still had enough strength to rip us both to pieces. However, its crippled leg and shoulder prevented it from reaching us. It stopped just inches below our feet.

-Your gamble had played off.

-Exactly. The little saint sitting on the branch next to me saved us both. If it wasn't for Maria's crippling blow to the Salamander's knee, we would have died right then and there. "You tricked me, little Victor" it said, with a strange calmness in its voice. I told the monster that it tricked me first, luring me back with another person, just so it could feast on two children instead of one… I looked at my sister and saw the blood on her fragile legs, where the monster's tail had hit. In that moment, my anger overwhelmed my fear and I threw my knife in the Salamander's open mouth, with unnatural precision and strength. It screamed in anger and fell out of the tree, spitting its glowing blood all over the ground. It looked at me and said: "We will see each other again, little human". I screamed with all my might then told the beast to count on it… It then quietly sank into the pond and disappeared under the murky waves. It was in that moment, I think, that I truly became a monster hunter. I overcame my fear. I felt invincible.

-Extraordinary! But you didn't kill it, did you?

-That was not the end of it, Madelyn. Now I was the hunter and it was the pray. The next morning, after my stepfather gave me a beating for missing church and then disappearing all day, I snuck into the police station, in the next village, and stole a pistol from one of the drunk policemen. My thieving skills form the previous years came in handy. It was a Russian made Tokarev, with an eight-round clip. Though I did not know it at the time, the Tokarev was an extremely powerful handgun. I got really lucky.

-What do you mean?

-You see, by the '80s, most of the Romanian communist police or "militia" as we called them, used the small caliber Carpati pistol, fabricated in our country. But this being a backward old station in a small rural area, the issuing of the newer, "safer" and more precise handguns was not completed... So, I got my hands on an old issue Russian hand canon. It took me a whole afternoon to figure out how it worked. I went deep into the woods and test-fired a round into an old tree. It kicked like a mule, almost jumping out of my hands, but it did the trick. I now had a basic understanding of how to hold it and aim it. That night I climbed the willow and waited for the Salamander to crawl out of the pond. I did not have to wait long. As soon as it raised itself on two feet and started tasting the air with its tongue, I noticed that all the wounds were healed.

-Magnificent beast.

-Yes, magnificent and hard to kill. I knew in that instant that I could not allow it to live, now that it caught the scent of human blood. I had to strike fast and hard. I yelled and taunted it from my high branch and it went for me immediately. I had a few seconds to strike before it reached me. The first round echoed into the night, making the cold air vibrate. I had missed, but not by much. The second bullet hit the Salamander in the head. It was too close for me to miss. It dropped like a stone and hit the ground with a loud thump. It wasn't dead. It started desperately crawling towards the pond, towards safety. I was now dominating the scene and my prey, taken by surprise, was fighting to stay alive. I fired off a couple of more rounds, hitting it in the back. When I realized it stopped moving, I quickly climbed down the tree and observed it from a safe distance. "Well done, little

Victor'' it suddenly said, calmly. There was no discernible emotion in the monster's words.

-Wouldn't expect anything else from a creature like that.

-I got closer. That was a foolish mistake. It suddenly wiped its massive tail and knocked me to the ground. It hit my chest like a club and knocked the wind out of me... But, I didn't drop my gun and I fired two more rounds, from the ground. One missed and the second hit the beast in the chest, causing blood to splash all over my feet. It now had four bullets in it and it was still slowly crawling towards the pond. I had just one round left, to finish the job. I walked up to my prey, gun in hand, and just before my final bullet hit its skull, it said: ''This is just the beginning, little hunter''. It was recognizing me for what I now was...

-A hunter. You played the helpless little kid card well.

-Yes, I outmaneuvered the monster at every turn, but I also got lucky... Still, it was my first true kill. The first of many.

-Let me guess: That's a story for another time.

-Yes.

-But wait, what did you do with the body? What about the gun?

-I beheaded the beast using my knife, just to make sure it wasn't going to get up again. I took one of its claws as a souvenir, then dragged the remains to the pond and pushed them in. I tossed the gun in as well. I wanted no evidence left behind. I gathered all the cartridges and even got rid of my blood-stained pants.

-So, there's no evidence of that ever happening...

-You still don't trust me, Madelyn? ...Here, take a look at this necklace. I've been wearing it ever since that day, to remind me of how I became a man.

-Is this...what I think it is?

-It's the Salamander's claw, the one I took that night.

-I've never seen anything like it. It's huge.

-Ant it's still sharp as a razor, even after all these years.

-Victor, I'm in awe. I thought...

-That all of this was just the elaborate fantasy of a madman?

-No, I mean...

-Keep it. Go have it analyzed if you wish. Just do it discreetly.

-I couldn't...

-Just take it. It will make our future sessions much easier if you trust me completely.

-Thank you, Victor. I feel like a little kid who just saw Santa, and he handed me a gift. I am ready to believe again.

-Just remember, tell no one where you got this and bring it back when you're done. I have to go now, Madelyn.

-I'll see you next week.

CHAPTER 5

THE FACELESS MONK

-Hello, Madelyn! You seem to be in a better mood this week.

-Hi, Victor! Are we alone?

-As always, I've sent my housekeeper away for the afternoon.

-So, I gave your...claw, to a trusted friend. He works in one of those high-tech forensic labs. He was able to run a DNA test on the thing.

-You seem excited. Well, what's the verdict?

-That's just it, there is no...verdict. The claw doesn't match anything in the database. It's like a whole new species. Furthermore, it has a strange type of DNA. Seems... alien. Frank was shaking when he handed it back to me. He said that he doesn't care where I got it from and he wants no further part in this. This, this is big, Victor.

-Calm down, my dear. This is big news to you, but it has been part of my reality for three decades.

-So, are there more of those things out there?

-Oh yes, many more. They are a shadow species. It's almost impossible for you humans to detect them. Their skin changes color like a chameleon's, they usually dwell deep underground and only come out to hunt... They are responsible for lots of missing person cases, especially in rural, isolated areas.

-How come we haven't discovered them by now?

-Who's "we", Madelyn? Mankind has known about these lizard-like creatures for millennia. But as time passed, sightings got rarer and stories turned into legends and myths.

You can find them mentioned in many cultures and religions, from Mayan to Christian.

-I mean us, modern age people with cameras, satellites, and all that high tech equipment.

-Your equipment doesn't detect them.

-Don't you mean "our" equipment?

-It's not what I use.

-Why doesn't it detect them?

-They camouflage themselves perfectly and are cold-blooded beasts. They don't show up on infrared sensors. Believe me, I've tried.

-Jesus! With claws like these, they must be killing machines.

-They would be more than a match for any solider, especially during the night. But they prefer to stay hidden.

-I'm getting scared here, Victor.

-They are not even the scary beasts, my dear. They are flesh and blood, well, sort-of. They can be shot and killed, as I have proven. The real scary monsters can't be harmed with knives and bullets.

-Are you going to tell me more about them, someday?

-As it so happens, our story takes us to one of those monsters.

-Ok, I'm actually not sure I want to know about these things, Victor. I'm afraid I won't be able to sleep at night anymore... I've been having these crazy nightmares since we met.

-I'm truly sorry, my dear. I haven't considered the impact my stories would have on you. That was... careless of me.

-No, there's no need to apologize. I came to your home and listened to your stories of my own volition. Well, not the first time, but you get the picture.

-I understand. Shall we continue, then?

-I... I think so. I'm not a little girl. I should be able to handle these things, right?

-My dear Madelyn, sometimes little girls can handle things just as well as adults.

-Your sister, stepsister, Maria, she was incredibly brave. What happened to her, after?

-Maria never told anyone about that night. She kept her promise to stay quiet. She... was a very special girl.

-Was?

-As brave as she was, she was very fragile.

-That only makes her braver.

-Unfortunately, she died of pneumonia, not one year later. I miss her every day, even though we only had a few years together. I still see her some days, you know. She's my guardian angel.

-Sounds like you loved her.

-My little sister, she was the first person I truly loved. She found me that morning, in the barn. She saved me twice, then she died. Life seems so unfair sometimes.

-Seems? So it's not really a random accident that she died so young?

-Nothing happens by accident, Madelyn, although it may appear that way to us.

-I still think that the death of an innocent young girl is a tragedy.

-Oh, I think so too, but sometimes tragedies need to happen. Life is not all about joy and pleasure.

-Ok, Victor. Please, continue with your story.

-After Maria died, things changed in the priest's household. A dark silence ruled over dinner every night. The priest tried to make peace with it, as if it was a lesson from God. Eventually, he came to believe that Maria's death was punishment for taking me in.

-Why would he ever think that?

-Like I said, he was a very perceptive person. He believed I was possessed by demons and brought destruction to his house. In a way, I guess he was right.

-What did he do with you?

-The next spring, he sent me away to live in a small monastery, to become a monk. One of his old friends was a hermit who lived in the woods, just outside the monastery walls.

-Is that even legal?

-I didn't ask about such things. I was just a boy. He packed my bags, gave me an old bible, new shoes, and sent me on my way.

It was a cold separation, but looking back I was never able to blame him. He was a good man.

-You don't seem to judge people very harshly. I like that.

-Maybe that's because I believe we are all fighting our own demons, Madelyn.

-Yes, I remember that lesson, from last time.

-Anyway, I saw the departure as the next stage in my evolution and embraced it wholly.

-And how was monastery life in late communist Romania?

-Very harsh indeed. As I'm sure you know, communists don't much appreciate religion, and the PCR was no different. They saw it as a mystical and superstitious education that undermined socialist values and took young people away from the workforce. Many tried to escape to the monasteries in the '50s, so the regime took measures against the church, confiscating lands, reducing work permits, and imposing strict rules to those who wished to become monks. All that, plus a propaganda campaign denouncing monastic life as a cancer to our communist way of life. Still, by the late '80s, monasteries were still standing, teaching, and preserving the monastic way of life.

-Yes, I sometimes find it miraculous how the church managed to survive all the dark tides of history.

-It managed to do so by the faith of those serving within the church, but also by strong pragmatic leadership.

-Pragmatists ruling over believers. That's a strange thing, isn't it?

-Strange but necessary if an institution of the soul and spirit is to survive in a world of earth and dust.

-That's the impression you give me, Victor. You seem to be a deeply spiritual person, but at the same time a practical and rational individual.

-It's a strange duality, I know. But this duality resides in us all. You will come to understand that it too is an illusion.

-I'm not sure I understand, but I'd like to hear about what happened to you in that monastery.

- Luca was a good teacher. After a short while, I understood that my being in his care was not an accident. The priest had sensed my true nature years before.

-This Luca, was he a monk?

-He was an old and wise one. He used to be a history professor before the communists came. He fled to the monastery to avoid being sent to a forced labor camp, as was the fate of many intellectuals back in the day. His wife had died decades ago and he never had any children. I guess he saw me as a son.

-He understood what you were?

-Not only understood, but experienced it himself. You see, he was a Touched, just like me. His house got bombed in the war and his wife died in his arms. He spent three days under the rubble before they finally found him, more dead than alive.

-That's how he became "touched"?

-Yes. It's also why he dedicated his life to finding others like him and reviving a millennia-old tradition that I was just finding out about: The "Solomonari Order"

-"Solomonari" as in King Solomon?

-You are very perceptive, Madelyn. The Solomonari are said to be an ancient order of Dacian priests, connected to the world of spirits. It was even rumored that they could control the skies above, calling down rain and storms.

-Seems like just a legend.

-It's more than just a legend, my dear. It's true that the modern world has no need for such mystics and wise men of the mountains, but even as recent as 100 years ago, they were a part of our reality.

-I guess the times moved on.

-Our perception of the world and its mysteries changed. Now, we praise science as the absolute truth, even though its priests are often godless materialists with no capabilities to think or imagine anything beyond their senses, their... data.

-We can't all be philosophers, Victor.

-That is true, but when we abandon the wonder and possibilities of worlds beyond our own, we limit ourselves to a pointless exercise of decomposing a mechanical reality. There is a great danger in that.

-The danger of becoming animals?

-Monsters, not animals, my dear. Animals live in balance with the world. We do not.

-So, the monster hunter of the future will slay humans, not beasts?

-What makes us human, if not our abilities to aspire towards the higher principles? If we abandon them, are we not beasts?

-Clever beasts.

-But still beasts, Madelyn. Our intellect is only a tool.

-And a dangerous one it is.

-Sharper than any claw, if wielded properly.

-It's the wielder that concerns you, right?

-The wielder's identity, yes. The master of the intellect.

-Victor, the more I talk to you, the more I realize I've not given much thought to such profound things. Maybe that's a mistake.

-The day we stop asking ourselves existential questions is the day we become animals.

-Or the day we finally get answers.

-Like I said, that day will never come while we are dressed in flesh and skin.

-So, did these Solomnari not have the answers, then?

-All they had were more pertinent questions and peace. I believe that asking the right questions sends us on the true path. What may lie at the end of it, must remain a mystery.

-So, Luca opened your eyes to all this stuff?

-He helped me to understand that a strong will and a tough hide are nothing without the principles to guide them. My mission to hunt the Red Girl would only be made harder if I refused to step back and understand why it was so important to me, in the first place.

-Did you ever get an answer to that question?

-I did, but many years later. That year, however, I uncovered another sinister clue to the puzzle of my existence.

-Here we go. The dark stuff begins.

-Indeed. One night, while I was walking alongside the old stone walls of the monastery, I saw a shadowy figure moving towards me. At first, I believed it was just a monk, returning home from a journey to the nearby village. As I got closer though, I realized the hooded figure did not touch the ground but floated inches above it. It stopped a few steps away from me and lowered its head. I couldn't see a face, because of the darkness. Then, it spoke: "Victor, She is coming". At first, I thought he meant the Red Girl, but then I sensed something different. He was not talking about a monster.

-How did you sense that?

-It's hard to explain. When entities talk to me, I hear and understand more than just the words. I sense meaning.

-Interesting.

-What I sensed this time chilled me to the bone. It was not evil. It was... nothingness. Vast, dark, cold nothingness. I sensed the desire to end all things, good and bad. That scared me more than the Salamander ever could. This... void, could not be bargained with. It wanted to conquer and obliterate... It was absolute.

-That sure sounds evil.

-That's just the thing, Madelyn, it didn't feel evil. It felt like the opposite of existence. It felt like the death of God's desire to exist.

-That's... the most frightening sentence I've ever heard in my life.

-At the time, I did not understand what was happening, but I heard him whisper a name, without words, as if even thinking it was to be done cautiously...

-Do I want to know? I feel like I don't. I'm getting strange chills, Victor.

-There is no turning back now, my dear.

-Ok, I trust you.

-That was the night I learned Her name, the ageless fear of all those who exist, good or evil: The Dark Mother.

-Who is She?

-She is the eternal night. Not a night of horrors but one of sterile nothingness.

-She sounds like the Anti-God.

-In a way, She is God, at least part of Him.

-What could you hope to achieve against such a force, Victor?

-I could achieve nothing, but I had a feeling… She was somehow connected to the Red Girl.

-Of course, it all leads back to her, doesn't it?

-Yes, it's the curse and blessing of my life, I suppose…

-What about the faceless monk?

-The robed monk, as you may have guessed, was an abomination himself. He was more than just a herald of the Dark Mother. He too was tainted by Urrud.

-He doesn't seem like the others.

-He was indeed different. Urrud only had a limited influence on him. The rest was just… a void. Not even demons could go there.

-Did he try to kill you?

-Sensing the corruption, I attempted to strike first. I threw my knife at the monk's chest, from a few steps away. At that range, it had enough force to split a brick in half but it flew right through him. The next thing I felt was a darkness in my mind and sight. I fell to the ground and lost consciousness, hitting my head on a rock.

-How did you survive the faceless monk, then?

-As it turns out, losing consciousness saved me from destruction. I later found out that the faceless monk was a lost Void Walker.

- Void Walker?

-An entity that walks between plains of existence, feeding on the fear of death, emanated from lesser creatures.

-Like us humans?

-Precisely. Losing consciousness meant it couldn't feed off me. Years later, when I learned to master my fear, the Void Walkers knew to steer clear of me.

-So they're not exactly monsters, are they?

-This one was, thanks to Urrud's corruption. Luca later told me that he tried to kill the faceless monk many times, but failed. I also found out that this abomination was feeding off the fear of doubtful monks, causing them to lose their way.

-To lose faith?

-Faith in a God that's both all-powerful and all-good. The classical Christian God.

-I don't think you believe in that God either.

-I don't, but shredding one's beliefs and replacing them with fear, mistrust, and confusion is an abominable thing to do, just for sport.

-I guess so. But how did you kill the faceless monk, in the end?

-Madelyn, I did not kill every monster I ever encountered, though not from a lack of trying. The faceless monk is on a shortlist of those who managed to escape me. There were others, as you will find out.

-Yes. All stories for another time, I presume?

-Everything in due time. See you next week, my dear.

CHAPTER 6

THE BEGGAR KING

-Hello, Victor.

-Good afternoon, my dear. Please, come in.

-I see you're redecorating.

-Yes, I'm trying to get rid of some unwanted memorabilia.

-Unwanted? How so?

-I admire your curiosity, Madelyn, but...

-Yes, yes! Don't say it.

-Hahaha! Tea?

-There's always good tea on your table, Victor.

-Well, I know lots of rare herbs.

- You must give me some tips.

-Certainly! I'll have Mary prepare a nice blend for you, next time.

-That's kind of you. So, have you given the book idea any more thought? I don't want to press you, but...

-I don't think a book is for me, Madelyn. I don't want all this to be dismissed as mere fiction, a story concocted for the entertainment of kids and grownups alike.

-It doesn't have to be a novel, you know. We could make it into a journal or an autobiography or...

-Please, let's just get back to the story, for now.

-Ok, Victor. As you wish.

-Last time I was telling you about my days at the monastery.

-Yes, I found that quite interesting. Especially that ancient order, the...''Solomonari''.

-Well, I didn't get a chance to study them in-depth. As it turns out, my days in the monastery were cut short. That first winter something happened, something big.

-Is that the winter of '89?

-Indeed. As you know, that period was one of great changes.

-Yes, the fall of the Soviet Union and the Berlin Wall, the Romanian revolution.

-Communism was no longer in fashion, it seems.

-Ha! Don't worry, I think it's making a comeback. The left has gone crazy these past few years... All that political correctness bullshit and all those social justice morons who have no clue what world they live in!

- Do you, Madelyn?

-I think I have a better understanding than those lazy unemployed punks or those "gender-fluid" people who think the world owes them something, just because they identify as pink hermaphrodite unicorns.

-I have no interest in politics, my dear. I've learned long ago that politics has just one goal: power... Left, right, middle, black or white, it doesn't matter. It's all the same: Just tribes of people being manipulated by hypocrites who only desire power.

-Wow! So you just declared my job useless. Worse than useless actually, since I probably work at spreading the lies. Am I right?

-Quite the contrary. Truth is important and you're not a liar, are you, Madelyn?

-No, I'm not.

-The problems usually appear when truth meets belief. We each have our own beliefs, I suppose, and that's fine. What's not fine, in my view, is others trying to rule by using those beliefs against us. That is monstrous behavior indeed.

-Yes, I know you think all politicians are monsters. What's stopping you from taking your hunt to that level, then?

-Good question! Like I've said, each of us has their own demons to fight. However, humans are still free to choose, changing their behavior over time.

-Victor, politicians rarely change, and it's usually not for the better.

-That may be, but their soul is not mine to banish and their spirit is their own. The monsters I hunt are earthly shells possessed by corrupted spirits from beyond this Universe.

-Ha! I think I know a few democrats who fit that description quite well.

-You do? Well then, maybe I'll investigate.

-I know we're just joking around, but, Victor, I sometimes wonder if we're any better than those abominations you hunt.

-I believe we each serve a purpose in the Creator's plan.

-And the monsters don't?

-They serve a purpose in God's plan.

- Wait, so God is not the Creator?

-God is also the Creator, but the Creator is not God.

-I don't understand.

-Madelyn, all you need to know right now is that humans and monsters, the true monsters, are very different. Why God has allowed them to plague us, is still beyond my understanding, but they are not a natural part of this Universe.

-Ok, I can understand that: Natural and unnatural.

-It's not that simple, but now is not the time for philosophy.

-Then let's get back to your story. What happened in the winter of '89?

-Romania was changing. Foreign pressure was high and the dictator Ceausescu was overthrown.

-Yes, I guess it makes sense. Romania was a borderland between two massive areas of influence.

-It still is, three decades later, but we're not here to discuss geopolitics either. For a 13-year-old boy, it was all a bit mindboggling, at first. I did however understand that this change was expected to be a big one. The pressure and fear of communism were slowly dissolving, being replaced with the confusion necessary to kick-start decades of carefully planned pillaging of Romania's wealth, by the same communists, who now called themselves politicians and businessmen.

-So the change was not that big, after all.

-Human nature doesn't change, my dear. Not because we call ourselves democrats or republicans or communists.

-So, what did a 13-year-old monster hunter with no money do, to survive in those troubled times?

-Luca, my teacher and mentor, grabbed me one morning and said: "Victor, the country is free now! You must go to Bucharest and find a way out of here." You see, he had a friend in West Germany, in Berlin.

-How did he manage that?

-It was an old colleague, an anthropology professor who was able to escape the country in the '50s. The man was now well over 80, retired. They managed to keep in touch through mail, when the regime loosened its grip on old monks, I suppose. He sent Horatiu a letter, telling him about me and urging him to take me in.

-That old man really cared about you.

-He was a kind and gentle soul, but he was also sharp and quick to act when it mattered. Even though I only stayed with him for nine months, he taught me more than the priest did in three years.

-You still refused to search for your real father?

-Real? You mean biological.

-I get it. Still, you must have been tempted. You probably needed money.

-Luca handed me a box with his life savings. It was just some old jewelry that belonged to his wife and a little money. I accepted it, with tears in my eyes. He literally gave me everything of value he still possessed. I could see that he was happy to give those things away and watch them gain purpose once again.

-He didn't care much for material possessions, I suppose.

-Most monks don't. As he handed me the box, he said: "Just remember, true wealth comes from within". That stuck with me ever since.

-You seem to be doing pretty well, all things considered.

-That is...

- A story for another time, yes!

-I took the box and bought a train ticket to Bucharest, that January. I remember walking 15 kilometers to the train station, in the dead of winter. Even though I lived in the woods for two years, I've never felt more alone and scared than I did in those moments. A whole world of possibilities was opening up in front of me.

- And you didn't have Luca or your dad, to guide you through it all. That must have been difficult.

-I was more at home in the forest than I was in society. Still, I spoke well, was polite, and had a decent understanding of how people think. "Empathy is the key to living out there", Luca always said.

-That is true, I suppose. How did you get to Berlin, though?

-I arrived in Bucharest that afternoon. The city looked like a grey ruin, full of strange people and noises. I had never seen a big city so I had nothing to compare it with. The spirits were restless there. I didn't like it. That night, I slept in the train station, on a broken wooden bench.

-No one helped you?

-No one cared. The whole city seemed shocked and confused. The second night was the beginning of one of my most difficult hunts.

-Finally! What was it this time?

- On the second day I ran around trying to find a bus that would take me to the border with Hungary, as Luca instructed, but everything was in chaos. I found a few leads but returned to my bench cold, hungry, and disappointed. Then, as I was about to lie down, I saw him: A tall dark figure with long red hair and a long red beard. Beggars and stray kids were flocking around him like he was some sort of savior.

-Who was he?

-That's what I was planning to find out. I sensed the same energy I usually felt, when in the presence of a monster. He behaved like some sort of prophet, some sort of beggar king. He sat on a bench and invited us all to sit down around him and listen. He went on to tell us that we were lost and forgotten, that the government and other people didn't care about any of us. He told us that we needed to take things by force, if we are to survive.

-That doesn't sound good.

-He continued, saying that we were owed payment for our suffering, payment in blood. He opened his heavy leather jacket and pulled out a bunch of knives. He handed them out to the people around him and said, in a somber voice: ''Thake these knives and exact your vengeance upon the world. Bring me the bloodied blades as evidence, and you shall be rewarded''.

-Did you take a knife?

-I did not. I was hiding in the back, trying to not get spotted by the Beggar King. But I failed. His eyes met mine and he stopped cold, in the middle of a sentence. He instantly knew who and what I was. Urrud's corruption was burning in his dark eyes. He paused for a few moments and then spoke to me alone, without words: "Little hunter, I could have you killed with just a word, should I desire it... I do not. But you, you wish to see me dead... I admire that". There was almost a hint of compassion in his declaration.

-That sounds so sinister. So, if he did not have you stabbed to death, I imagine he had other plans for you.

-The tall figure slowly walked towards me, as the others stepped aside, knives in hands. He placed his cold bony hand on my forehead and handed me an old rusty knife: "Take it. You have just as many reasons to be angry as any of them.", he said in a soft voice, for everyone to hear. I pushed his hand back and took out my own knife, showing it to him. "No, thank you", I said. The Beggar King smiled and replied, in an even softer voice: "Tell me, child, are you hungry?" He pulled out a small chocolate bar and handed it to me, as the others watched in envy. "Go on, eat!", he urged me. I could sense agitation around me. When I looked at that chocolate it took all my strength to refuse it... I was starving.

-That must have angered him.

-Yes, he immediately changed his tone. Refusing his charity made him furious. His hand was shaking and his eyes were glowing with rage.

-You declared firmly, in front of everyone, that you did not depend on him, no matter what. You undermined his authority.

-Precisely. I almost didn't, but I guess my pride was marginally victorious over my hunger and desperation. The Beggar King then raised his hand, as if to signal the other to leave. They all disappeared into the night, in mere seconds. He lowered his burning eyes towards me and said: "You are stubborn, little hunter. Let's see how long your resolve will last"... He then unwrapped the candy bar, took a big bite and threw it in the trash. Before I could make a move, he faded into the darkness, laughing.

-I can't even begin to imagine what you went through, Victor.

-Even after he left, I was tempted to reach into that bin and grab the chocolate... I didn't. Instead, I made a plan to trap and kill the abomination. The following night, as the beggars were flocking around him, presenting their bloodied knives and receiving pieces of moldy bread in exchange, I ran out into the cold and stole a roll of heavy telephone cable, from a warehouse nearby. I hid in the warehouse that night and knitted a large net, using the cable. It must have weighed at least 10 kilograms. I dragged it back to the train station, early the next morning, and tied it to a metal beam, high over the Beggar King's bench. I waited for him to return the next night but he didn't. His acolytes became restless and desperate. They started to vandalize the station and the surrounding blocks, taking advantage of the general disarray in the city. Eventually, some police showed up and the Beggar King's army scattered.

-But where was he?

-He just disappeared... Or so I thought. I saw him again days later, after I finally managed to sell some of the jewelry to buy food. He led a group of policemen into a warehouse, sneaking as quietly as possible, just after sunset. I followed them and saw the group meeting with a few men, who played the police in large chunks of dollar bills. From what I could hear, the three men controlled all the warehouses in the neighborhood, plus an old factory.

-But why did they need the police?

-They were obviously trying to sell the factory for scrap, while also selling the stocks in the warehouses, profiting from the mayhem and corruption.

-Who were these men?

-They looked like a bunch of high ranking communists, to me. Of course, they were now "venture-capitalists", just a month after the PCR lost power. They needed the police to patrol the neighborhood, preventing the looting of their... assets. Assets that in fact belonged to the government.

-I get it, but what did any of this have to do with the Beggar King?

-I suspect that the Beggar King was running the whole show, from the shadows. You see, he created the mayhem, the violence, and the looting. He made the area cheap and undesirable so that the communist parasites could profit, but he also made paying off the cops a necessity. He sowed the seeds of corruption all around, turning theft, bribery, and violence into business as usual. I don't know if he had any interest beyond that, but everyone seemed to be afraid of him, like he held a great and terrible power over them... He now reminds me of Ceausescu's "Securitate", the state agency that maintained communist power through absolute fear.

-That's incredible. Did you manage to kill him?

-My silly trap was obviously not going to work, so I abandoned the whole idea. Killing the Beggar King was going to be difficult, because he moved around a lot, spreading his tainted influence throughout the city. He was also followed by his minions almost everywhere. I stalked him for weeks, but I soon ran out of food and places to hide... I eventually had to stop.

-So you just moved on?

-I needed to reach Berlin if I was going to keep my promise to Luca. But I never forgot about this monster. I vowed to return to Bucharest someday, to find him and destroy him.

-Did you? And please, please don't tell me that this is a story for another time! I need to know!

-If you must know, I returned to Bucharest 12 years later to continue the hunt. It took me months to track him down, following the trail of corruption. He was now involved in organized crime and money laundering, still using violence and manipulation as his main tools.

-Please tell me that you killed that son of a bitch.

-I put a crossbow bolt in the back of his skull from three feet away. Of course, he wasn't exactly human so that didn't kill him. It just weakened him long enough for me to soak him in gasoline and light him up. He burned for twenty minutes, laughing and rolling in the dirt. When it was all done, all that was left of him were the knives. He must have kept them as trophies... Who knows how much blood those blades had seen.

-Incredible! You were a much better hunter, after all that time.

-I was 25, by then I had banished many abominations like him, almost dying twice in the process.

-Stories for another time?

-Perhaps.

-Sometimes I get the feeling that you're not telling me everything, Victor.

-I have my reasons... I'll see you next week, my dear. I have some business to attend to right now.

-Ok, Victor. Please give that book idea some more thought.

CHAPTER 7

THE OVERSEER

-Hello, Victor. It's good to see you.

-Good to see you too, my dear. Please, come in!

-Wow! Your house is empty. Are you redecorating or moving?

-Sometimes, in order to make room for the new, you have to let go of the old. Wouldn't you say?

-I guess so.

-Ah! Mary has prepared the herbal blend I promised.

-You didn't have to, Victor.

-Oh, but I did! So, how are you, Madelyn?

-To be honest, not so good.

-I'm sorry to hear it.

-I haven't been getting much sleep lately... I've been having strange dreams again.

-Strange dreams you say? Anything in particular?

-Yes, actually. This woman in black robes keeps appearing to me. It's like a recurring theme.

-Does she speak to you?

-She never says a single word. She carries this bronze hourglass with golden sand in her hands. She shows it to me, scratching on the glass with her long black nails.

-I see... Anything else?

-She always breaks the hourglass. She lets the sand flow through her palms and down to her feet. Then, she steps on it and it turns from gold to lead, before disappearing completely. It feels so real, Victor. It scares the shit out of me.

-Poor thing! Perhaps I can help. As luck would have it, the herbal blend Mary has prepared for you is quite soothing and can probably help with your sleep problems.

-You think so? I mean, at this point I'd try anything.

-Just give it a try and we'll see.

-Ok. Thank you. So, you think my dreams have anything to do with our talks?

-Perhaps. The human mind is a fascinating thing. Your subconscious must have picked up on some signals.

-Wow!

-What is it?

-I thought that you of all people would have an explanation that's a bit more... supernatural. Instead, you're basically saying that I'm crazy. My mom says the same thing, you know.

-What about your dad? What does he think?

-He left us when I was a teenager.

-It seems that you had your share of hardships, my dear.

-I guess, but I'm not complaining. He did leave us lots of money... Enough to pay for my education and an apartment on Park Avenue.

-Regardless, no amount of money can replace a lost parent.

-How did you know he was lost?

-Was I wrong?

-He mysteriously disappeared about ten years ago, right when I got into college.

-That is unfortunate.

-Yeah, well, he was a mysterious guy. He mostly kept to himself.

-What did your mother think about that?

-She didn't seem to mind. There was no love lost between them.

-What did your father do?

-Oh, he owned a chain of antique stores and pawn shops all over Brooklyn. He came to America when he was very young, and I guess that trade made sense to him.

-Interesting... I guess it's time to continue with our stories.

-I guess so.

-Last time I told you about my arrival in Bucharest, right after the revolution.

-Yes, I found that whole business with the Beggar King to be quite disturbing. Good thing you managed to kill him, in the end.

-Ah, yes! About that, here's one of the Beggar King's knives. I took it off him as a souvenir, after I ended him.

-I take it you have quite a large souvenir collection.

-Well, I'm trying to reduce it to a bare minimum, as of late.

-You want me to keep the knife?

-If you wish.

-It's a creepy, rusty, blackened kitchen knife. Why would I want it?

-I think we all need subtle reminders of the true nature of this world, especially the sinister bits.

-That may be, but I still don't want an antiquated murder weapon in my house, and it seems like you don't either.

-I was planning on getting rid of it. I no longer need trinkets to remind me of monstrosities. My senses are sufficient.

-Yeah, it seems you have become quite the minimalist.

-Anyway, let's get back to the story... After I was done chasing the Beggar King, I spent my days roaming the streets in search of anyone that would help me. It was a grim period in the city's history.

-I imagine it was chaos.

-Organised chaos, Madelyn... You see, in a ruthless attempt to consolidate his new power, one of Ceausescu's old enemies, Ion Iliescu, called upon the coal miners of Jiu Valley to pacify the angry population. At that time, young people hoping for a better future, along with what remained of Romania's historical parties, were protesting against the same old communists taking over. Iliescu wanted them gone. He called upon the miners, the rough, hardened, and hateful cave dwellers to "save the country" from the hippies and students who were trying to sink it into anarchy. It was a bloody lie and it led to a blood bath. This happened twice before the elections that got Iliescu his power and several times after that. Every time the miners came, armed with clubs and thick metal cables, they cracked heads open and filled the streets with innocent blood. These atrocities far surpassed the actual revolution in body counts.

-Jesus! It must've been terrifying.

-It was as terrifying as any monster. Back then, I had no idea what was going on... Now, it's not the hateful, ignorant individual acts themselves that shake me but the lies, the monstrous lies.

-Lies beget monsters, I suppose.

-If there is one living soul that closely resembles a monster, then Iliescu is right up there, on the shortlist of candidates.

-He still lives? Imprisoned, I suppose.

-No, he walks freely. It seems that the inconvenient truths of our past are still too hot to address publically, in any definitive manner.

-You mean to say that reopening those old wounds would have consequences for powerful people.

-Something like that. But the past still haunts us. It will continue to do so because those old wounds have turned into scars.

-Not the kind of scars that one wears proudly, I presume.

-There were plenty of heroes in those times, Madelyn. Their scars are not hidden but continue to be ignored.

- The more we talk, the more I am convinced that humanity is doomed, Victor. I could use some hope right now.
-Well, let's get on with my story, then. As luck would have it, after some weeks of sleeping in the gutter and avoiding angry miners, I ran across a group journalist from West Germany. As you may recall, the Berlin Wall fell in November 1989 and, as the wind of change was blowing through Europe, reporters came to assess the situation in our country. The view was a grim one: poverty, confusion, broken families, and orphans. In spite of all that, people gained renewed hope that their lives would improve.
-But that wasn't going to happen anytime soon.
-The country could certainly change for the better, considering the existing infrastructure and the lack of external debt. But things were in "transition", and that meant a new pecking order was being cemented. Unfortunately, as I said, the fight for power and resources had nothing to do with the desire to improve the lives of Romanians and everything to do with who got to buy, steal or pillage what was owed to the people. Fortunes were made in mere years. I'm talking millions and even billions of dollars. Those who met the new political regime with money and influence got everything, while the honest working people got stiffed, as usual. It was truly the Wild West for a few years... Billions of dollars left the country while our "fresh start" was purchased with borrowed money, that the poor would have to pay for decades to come.
-Yes, the same old story: The poor get poorer and the rich get richer.
-Precisely, but here it happened even quicker, since corruption rooted itself deep in every government after '89, and privatization of state-owned assets meant everything was for sale, often in dubious circumstances.

-So, your German reporters, did they help you?

-They came to report about our orphans, amongst many other things. I told them my story, leaving out all the supernatural elements, of course. I didn't tell them my father was alive and they didn't ask. They read the letter Luca had received from Horatiu. I asked them to take me to Berlin and, after making a few phone calls, they concluded that it couldn't be done legally. I was 13 at the time. I didn't even have proper id.

-They did help you though.

-They gave me a couple of hundred German marks and arranged for me to stay with a friend of theirs, in Bucharest, promising to return and aid me further. I needed to be at least 14 to get a proper id and passport.

-So, you had one more lovely year to spend in Bucharest.

-It appeared so... Alexandra, the widow who was helping me, attempted to send me to school. But when she realized I had to be institutionalized or sent back to my adoptive father, she gave up on that idea.

-So, what did you do?

-I studied. I now had access to better books, you see. Alexandra was kind enough to help me. Her husband had died in the revolution and she attempted to find meaning in her life.

-Did you run into any monsters?

-No, there was no time. Later that summer, Alexandra got a phone call from our journalist friends in Berlin. They managed to get a hold of Horatiu, Luca's old friend, who was well connected and quite rich. He found an elegant solution to get me to Berlin. You see, he got remarried shortly after leaving Romania, in the '50s, and fathered two children... Unfortunately, Anna, his 38-year-old daughter couldn't have children of her own. Apparently, she tried for a whole decade and failed. She and her husband desperately wanted a child but, at their age, came to understand that adoption was the only way. They weren't prepared to deal with toddlers anymore, so, adopting a 13-year-old boy would be like skipping all that and magically getting a smart, educated teenager.

-Is that what you were?

-That is how Luca described me to his old friend.

-But wait, couldn't they've just adopted a German kid?

-I think that adopting a German kid would have been easier, since it would have eliminated the language barrier. I don't know about the bureaucracy involved, however. Years later I found out that Horatiu didn't push them in my direction. Anna wanted to connect with her father, somehow. She believed that a Romanian child would help with that. She even spoke a bit of Romanian.

-That's amazing luck on your part, I guess.

-I don't believe it was luck, my dear. Anyway, as soon as I found out that the adoption process had begun, I started learning German from some old manuals Alexandra procured for me. When the papers where all done, later that year, I already spoke a bit and was able to have a basic conversation with my new adoptive mother. I won't bore you with all the details of adoption and my difficulties adjusting to Berlin.

-It doesn't seem like you have any difficulties adjusting to anything, Victor.

-It's sufficient to say that I was fluent in German by the end of next year. Horatiu paid for me to get home-schooled during that time, so I could start high school in Berlin, like any normal German teenager.

-Let me guess, you excelled at learning and amazed everyone.

-Quite right. More to the point, I was able to roam the streets of Berlin during the night, hunting for monsters.

-Sounds like your new parents were quite permissive.

-Not really, but then again they mostly didn't know about my night-time activities. While spending time with me and Horatiu, they got a sense of family... You see, by the time I got to Berlin, the unification of Germany had just been completed. I knew it was a big deal because everyone just wouldn't stop talking about it. As you may know, that was a time when many German families got reunited. Perhaps my new family needed to experience a bit of that joy.

-It makes sense. The world was changing and they wanted to change with it.

- Yes, and I was interested in what the world was changing into. I needed to know what shapes my future enemies would take. The Berlin Wall, which had fallen figuratively the previous November, was still very much a present landmark. So was the desolate no man's land that accompanied many portions of the border. I used to walk through there at night, to try and get a sense of my new environment.

-It didn't feel like home, did it?

-Madelyn, I never really felt at home anywhere. That is just one of my many curses...

-So, what did you think of your new environment?

-I had heard stories about what had happened and I was somehow connected to it all. The spirits I sensed made sure of that. However, my mind was constantly seeking the chilling energies of Urrud's minions. I knew that they would eventually find me, wherever I went.

-So you needed to find them first.

-The wall reeked of negative energies. I knew that the monsters would flock to it, attempting to profit from the decades fear, anger, and suffering that were now deeply embedded into the cold concrete itself.

-Do they usually do that?

-They do. But as of late, they are becoming more and more cunning. It's getting harder to detect them.

-Even for you?

-Even for me. But we will get to that part later. Back in Berlin, I had just discovered a trace of anguish that would lead me to my next monster encounter. This time, however, the energies were stronger than anything I had ever encountered.

-Seems like every monster you fight is stronger than the last.

-Strength is a relative notion. Some are more powerful, some more devious and some have an intellect that far surpasses that of any human. This particular entity was a dangerous combination of many traits.

-What was it?

-After following the clues for several nights, I stumbled upon an old building, near the wall. It appeared abandoned at first glance, but after staking out the site I noticed that people were occasionally going in and coming out, just before sunset and shortly after sunrise. One night, I noticed a large raven flying away from one of the broken windows, on an upper floor. As soon as I saw it I felt a jolt of powerful energy hitting me in the chest. It was an unusual experience, even for me.

-How do you mean?

-It didn't feel like the mark of Urrud. It had less violence but more... darkness.

-I'm not sure I understand.

-I didn't understand either, but it seemed like I had discovered a new ancient entity, one whose intentions I knew nothing about.

-It certainly doesn't sound like good news, the fact that there are more of these demons out there.

-I just call them "Elders". I'm not sure that their behavior upon this plain is indicative of their true nature.

-So tell me about this one's behavior.

-The next day, I went to the building just before sunset, like all the others. There were already people gathered upfront, whispering about someone they called the Overseer. He sounded like an ominous figure. Half an hour later, the large wooden door opened and we all heard a deep, somber voice: "Please, come in", it said. The people around me were scared and happy at the same time, making me properly confused.

-But you entered the building anyway.

- Naturally, I went in with all of them, making sure to hide somewhere in the back. As we stepped inside, I saw a large lobby filled with old paintings, mostly portraits. The air was damp and cold, filling our lungs with the smell of rot and mold. Suddenly, a massive figure appeared at the head of the large wooden staircase. It was a man in his 50's, with a comically large mustache, a chin like a Neanderthal, and eyes as black as coal. He wore a policeman's uniform, a high ranking one by the look of it.

-Sounds like a proper monster already.

-He instructed us to come up one at a time and step into his office. The people quickly formed a row, reluctant to take the first spots. I obviously placed myself at the back of the line, to buy more time and find out who this Overseer really was.

-What did the people tell you?

-Most of them were East Berliners, seeking help. They needed someone connected to aid them in their quest for a better life, now that the city was united. They talked about the Overseer as being some sort of god-like figure, who knew everybody and everything.

-Was he?

-Rumour had it that he used to be an influential police chief in West Berlin. After being involved in a corruption scandal, he mysteriously disappeared, leaving no clue to his whereabouts or intentions. He resurfaced after the wall fell, almost two years later, but he wasn't the same man... Not even his family recognized him.

-Someone or something got to him.

-That was my theory as well. I understood that he became lost and was now possessed by a powerful Elder. That made him more dangerous than any of Urrud's minions, since I had no clue about what I was getting myself into.

-Didn't the people tell you more?

-They were reluctant to talk. They warned me that the Overseer was always watching... After a while, I noticed that not all of the people climbing the stairs would come back down. Those who did looked terrified and didn't say a single word to the rest of us... After what seemed like forever, it was finally my turn to go up. I was all alone in that cold dark lobby when I heard his voice, echoing through the halls: " Are you going to keep me waiting, Victor?"

-Naturally, he knew your name. I think I would have pissed myself right then and there.

-You never know what you are capable of, my dear, until you are faced with brutally hard choices. That night, running was not an option. I felt it. I was shaking as I was slowly climbing the stairs, leading up to the first-floor atrium. Each step I took made me more composed and determined. There was no turning back... I mustered all my strength to hide the fear.

-You must have been the bravest 13-year-old alive.

-I doubt that. As I reached the Overseer's office, I had abandoned all illusions about myself and made peace with the fact that I would no longer be in control of my life, once I stepped through that dark oak door. It was the first time I had ever felt that strangely peaceful sentiment... I finally stepped inside and saw the Overseer sitting behind a massive oak desk, decorated with what appeared to be the signs of the zodiac. A single faint lamp lit the whole room in a pale orange color. I saw books everywhere, even on the floor. The Overseer pointed to a small chair on my side of the desk and I sat down without saying a single word. He then opened a massive book with dark bronze covers and proceeded to flip quietly through the pages. This went on for a while, but I dared not say anything... Finally, without even looking at me, he said: "Victor Rotaru, what do you need form me?". His calm and unpassionate tone threw me off my game. It relaxed me and encouraged me to become strangely daring in my reply: "I want to know who you are.", I said boldly. The Overseer laughed, appearing genuinely amused. He then replied, while writing something in his giant notebook: "You know, most people come to me because they have no choice. They come to me because they are sinners. You, little Victor, are not yet a sinner." He then paused for a few seconds and continued, lifting his eyes off the paper for the first time, to meet mine: "What do you truly desire, my child?". His dark eyes now appeared like marbles of polished black onyx, flickering with the faint light of the lamp...

-I love how vivid your memories are, Victor.

-Yet another one of my curses, I assure you.

-What was your answer?

-The second time, I gave my reply a lot more thought, searching the full depth of my soul. I realized there could only be one answer but, before I had a chance to utter a single word, the Overseer smiled and said: "You need to find her, don't you?" There was no need to elaborate. We both knew who he was talking about... I felt chills running down my spine.

-The Red Girl.

-Indeed. I felt my heart race as I slowly nodded my head, indicating my response to the Overseer. He lowered his eyes to the paper once again and started to write something. Minutes passed before he spoke: "It will cost you, Victor. If you want to find her, you need to do something for me first." I immediately thought to myself that I would never agree to any of his twisted demands, fearing for my soul. Of course, the abomination sitting across the desk sensed my answer before I could utter it and continued: "I usually stay out of Urrud's business and he stays out of mine. If I am to aid you, it would complicate things. I do not like to complicate things. Do you, Victor?". His question didn't require my answer... "I need you to aid me by performing a simple task", he said, like he was about to ask me to get him a pack of cigarettes.

-I'm guessing it wasn't quite that easy.

-He wrote down an address for me and then placed a large metal disc on the table. He said that all I had to do was to take the disc to that address and place it inside the house, hidden. Apparently, the Overseer knew all about my breaking and entering skills. The job seemed simple and harmless enough, so I immediately became suspicious. I wanted to ask why but, as usual, he was one step ahead of me. He told me that the police chief's family lived in that house. His wife cheated on him for years. After he disappeared, she married the current, freshly elected police chief. He told me that the man was corrupt and that he had climbed his way to the top by working for the Soviets and sabotaging his adversaries in the police force.

-So the Overseer wanted revenge?

-No, I don't think he cared about the problems of his... host.

-Don't tell me that he was seeking justice, because I don't believe that for a second.

-Neither did I, because he never lied to me. He told me that the disc was radioactive and it would make the chief and the wife suffer immensely before reaching a much-deserved end. The Overseer was a tormentor, you see.

-Don't tell me that you actually did it.

-It was a very difficult choice. On the one hand, I knew that the couple had cheated, lied, and stolen, affecting the lives of countless people. They were well deserving of punishment. I also knew that finding the Red Girl again, without the Overseer's help, would be a monumental task, requiring years of work and dedication. Even so, there would be no guarantees of success. It seemed like I was given a unique opportunity to fulfill my vows and perhaps save humanity from Urrud's corruption. On the other hand, I had to commit murder in the ugliest manner possible. Could I even live with that?

-Couldn't you at least attempt to hunt the Overseer and force him to tell you the Red Girl's location? Isn't that what you do?

-My dear Madelyn, as soon as I walked into that office I realized that the Overseer was far beyond anything I had witnessed. How do you hunt someone who is aware of your every thought and knows what you are about to do before you yourself realize it?

-Good point... Seems impossible.

-Not impossible, as it turns out, but damned near to it for a 13-year-old boy with no experience in such matters.

-So, did you do it? Did you kill the police chief and his wife?

-I sat there in silence for minutes, deciding what to say. While I was debating the situation with myself I realized that the Overseer was enjoying my thoughts, like a show. In the end, I didn't need to utter an answer. He did it for me: "Pity, I really thought that you were stronger, Victor." He said those words in a sober tone, without looking at me. He then told me to return to him, if I decide to agree to his proposal.

-That's it? He just let you go?

-He didn't have any further business with me, but he would have gladly used me, had I accepted the deal.

-What about all those other people visiting him? What happened to them?

-I'm not quite sure. I imagine they made their deals in order to get the lives they wanted. Many of them disappeared forever, as I later found out. I knew then that Sassom was using them to build his own army of the Lost, just like Urrud.

-Wait, who is this Sassom?

-Before I left, the Overseer saw fit to answer my first question. He was called Sassom the Dark. After I finally left the building, the doors closed behind me and the light on the first floor went out. A few minutes later I saw the large raven again, flying away into the night. That was Sassom leaving his vessel to conduct his business elsewhere.

-So, this Sassom the Drak, he seems different than Urrud.

-Oh yes, very much so! While Urrud is interested in spreading his corrupt energies, Sassom feeds off the guilt, pain, and fear of those he judges to be damned. He is also instrumental in acquiring vast amounts of information about the places and people he visits, aiding him in his quest to spread the suffering of humanity. I believe he sees us as a doomed species, weak and prone to failure.

-But he did spare you... Why is that?

-Sassom didn't see me as a threat, however, he did see something in me. I'm not sure exactly what, but it stopped him from harming me... As I said, I don't claim to fully understand these Elders.

-Did you ever encounter him again?

-I did, but that is a story for another time.

-I don't know why I even asked.

-I'll see you next time, my dear. Don't forget your tea.

-Sure! Goodbye, Victor.

CHAPTER 8

THE DREAM SLAYER

-Hello, Victor... Sorry for being late. I ran into a little trouble in traffic.

-You look pale, Madelyn. I take it my herbal remedies haven't done the job.

-They actually helped, but my troubles run a little deeper than sleep deprivation.

-Well then, perhaps we should spend some time talking about that, if you wish. Please, sit down.

-I don't know how to say this, Victor, but I don't think I can keep our appointments anymore. I have some trouble in my personal life, not to mention at work, and I don't think our meetings are helping. To be honest, I'm more than a little freaked out.

-What's wrong? I feel like we don't talk that much about you. You have learned so many things about me, yet I know so little about you.

-Yeah, well, I'm not that interesting. Believe me.

-I'm not sure I agree. You seem to be extremely sensitive to...

-Yeah?

-To a certain type of energy, let's say.

-What is that supposed to mean?

-When I first met you, you were strong, defiant even. Being here and talking to me seems to have affected more than your mood.

-Speaking of my mood, could you please just say what you mean? I'm not capable of deciphering Victor-talk right now.

-I believe you may be in danger, my dear. Our last conversation, your dream, they got me worried.

-You said that the dream was just my mind playing tricks on me. Am I going insane?

-No, on the contrary, you are beginning to see things more clearly. But you do have your weaknesses.

-And what exactly am I seeing, Victor?

-This may be difficult for you to understand... Perhaps you are right. Perhaps we should stop the interviews, for now.

-So, you're just giving up on me?

-I thought that's what you wanted.

-Never mind what I said. If you know something that may help, I want to hear it. Why am I in danger? Is someone after me?

-I'm not sure yet.

-Can you please just give me a straight answer, for once?

-I wish I could, my dear. First, let's talk a bit about the problems you've been having.

-What about them?

-When did they begin, exactly?

-Let's see... About the time I've begun having weird dreams, I suppose. Since then, strange things started happening. It's like something bad is following me everywhere.

-What makes you say that?

-My crazy ex-husband is back in town, for one. He seems more sociopathic than usual.

-I didn't know you were married.

-I was very young. It only lasted a couple of years.

-Any kids?

-No, like I said, we were very young.

-I understand. Have people started to act strange around you?

-Yes, they have. At work and at home.

- I see...

-It's like everyone has given up on me, on life, on... everything.

-Thank you, Madelyn. That's all the information I needed. I urge you to remain calm. I will have more information for you next time we meet.

-You think I'm safe, for now?

-You are quite safe. It's probably just a spirit that needs to be driven away.

-And are you going to drive it away?

-Perhaps. It's too soon to tell. You will have to remain optimistic.

-I feel a little better knowing you're on the job, Victor... Thank you.

-Don't thank me yet, my dear. In the meantime, shall we continue with the story?

-Yes. Maybe that will help me get my mind off things... Unless of course your story is sinister and professing the impending doom of humanity. Oh, wait...

-I find it's always best to know, no matter how harsh the reality.

-I suppose you're right.

-So, last time I told you about my encounter with the ancient entity called Sassom the Dark.

-Yes, cheerful fella. Made Urrud sound like an amateur.

-I'm not sure we can compare the two. Our understanding of them is quite limited. To me, at that time, the punishment of the so-called "sinners" seemed less of a problem than the corruption of humanity.

-Urrud was still your number one enemy.

-Urrud was my only enemy, Madelyn. Other than myself, of course.

-What do you mean?

-Well, if Urrud had his way, I would be corrupted and turned into his champion. So, it would seem like my biggest enemy is in fact my own weakness.

-That's an interesting point of view. From this perspective, the monsters are just faces of yourself that he wishes you to see.

-You surprise me, Madelyn.

-Like you said, maybe I'm starting to see things more clearly.

-Indeed...

-Well? Are you going to tell me what abomination you encountered next?

-Yes. I called him the Dream Slayer. We all did, actually.

-All of who?

-The kids from school.

-So this monster was what, a teacher?

-In the most perverted and twisted sense of the word, yes.

-This should be interesting.

-As it turns out, the Dream Slayer, as sinister as he was, taught me one of the most valuable lessons of my life. He ended up being a teacher after all.

-I'm sure not all of your high school buddies would agree.

-That's a certainty...

-Who was he?

-He was a history teacher, one that used to be a college professor. He didn't teach my class but we discovered each other sometime after I started attending high school. He was always the last teacher to leave school and only taught in the evenings. His nickname, the Dream Slayer, was given by previous generations of kids. Even the teachers steered clear of him.

- Were they scared of him?

-He had power over them. They didn't mess with him and always accepted every proposal he made to the school board, no matter how absurd... There were rumors of missing kids and even teachers.

-How old was this guy?

-He appeared to be in his early 60's, but I heard teachers say that he had been teaching there since before any of them. No one knew his past.

-That's an indication of a monster, I take it.

-It is a sign, yes, when things don't add up. A kid once showed me a photo of an SS cornel who looked suspiciously like him. In the photo, he was shaking hands with Hitler himself. The photo didn't make any sense at first, since the Nazi officer appeared to be in his 50's, and that was 50 years before.

-So longevity is also a sign.

-Sometimes, yes. Of course, to properly function in society as mister Muller did, he would have needed to adopt forged identities. People would start to get suspicious if you look like a healthy 60-year-old man that was born more than a century before. Who knows how many lives he lived and how much harm he caused, spilling his lies.

-The nickname was well deserved, I take it.

-Indeed it was. Mister Muller didn't grade his students on how well they learned their lessons from the textbooks. He graded them on how well they were able to explain history according to his own viewpoints. He didn't ask what had happened, he asked why, until it all boiled down to who was superior and who was inferior, who was dumb or smart, who was chosen to lead and who was born to be enslaved.

-Sounds a lot like a certain doctrine.

-It was more than just propaganda to Mister Muller. He seemed to stand by his every word. He even divided his classes into superior and inferior students, sitting them as he saw fit and embarrassing the ones he deemed unworthy.

-That sounds terrible. Why didn't the school do anything about it? Weren't there any complaints?

-I suppose there were, but no one was acting on them. Mister Muller seemed to rule the entire neighborhood with an iron fist. He even managed to create a divide amongst teachers, separating them into favorable and unfavorable groups.

-I can't imagine how he would do that.

-The man's charisma was monstrously powerful. He dominated his classroom and he dominated the adults around him.

-He knew a lot.

-Yes, it probably helped that he was more than a century old and extremely skilled in the art of manipulation.

-Was he a pawn of Urrud?

-It was difficult to determine at first, since his energies were clouded in a powerful mist. He was an extremely devious entity. I managed to sneak into some of his classes to hear him speak. He had a magical way of molding everyone according to his will.

-Even you?

-Even I was tempted to adhere to his doctrines, since it appealed to my ego. As strong as I was, I still felt the need to be appreciated and valued by my peers.

-The need to feel superior, you mean.

-Perhaps. I was only 14 at the time, you mustn't forget. Mister Muller gave me one of his books and I read it. At first, I did it in the hope of learning more about my enemy, but I soon found myself bewitched by his alluring rhetoric.

-So, this monster was also an author.

-He wrote under a pseudonym and always printed the books himself. He never sold them in shops. He only gave them to his most promising students.

-But why did he give one to you?

-To attempt my corruption, of course.

- I can't imagine you falling for that shit.

-It was an extremely well documented and written treaty, describing social classes and races throughout history, in a whole new light. Truth mixed with belief and the metaphysical make for dangerous rhetoric... The scary part was that I could find few arguments to combat his theories. I imagine most adults would have trouble doing that, and we were just kids.

-Putty in his hands.

-Precisely.

-This is perhaps the most dangerous monster I've heard of yet, Victor. Poisoning the minds of young people like that must have had drastic consequences.

-The high school was prone to outbursts of violence. There were gang members lurking in the courtyard. They would spit on other teachers while treating Mister Muller like a king.

-I guess that explains how he kept the teachers in line.

-That was just one of the many ways he did it. He was also well connected in the police and even had a few influent politicians visiting his house, if rumors were to be believed.

-So, this ex-Nazi college professor turned undercover high school teacher was slowly gaining traction.

-Yes. His words were as dangerous as any weapon, justifying violence and other atrocities.

-I wonder how you finally got to him.

-He and I played a cat and mouse game for months. I concluded that the energetic mist that was covering his true nature from me was also hiding mine. We both suspected something was odd but didn't act on it until we were sure. One night, after I became convinced that Urrud's influence was present, I waited for the Dream Slayer to leave the schoolyard and followed him to his house. He always walked.

I was surprised to learn that le lived in a modest two-bedroom house, with no wife and kids. Just him and a whole bunch of cats... My plan was to accidentally bump into him on the street the next night and ask something about his new book, The Sacred Order. I heard about it from a bunch of skinheads, but Mister Muller was exceptionally secretive about his latest work. I knew he had a plan of sinister proportions and needed to investigate.

-It seems the hunter was now turning into a detective.

-I did as the situation demanded. You see, a monster like the Dream Slayer couldn't be defeated with steel alone. His work was more dangerous than the creature itself. If I was to defeat him, I needed to stop his poison from spreading to the streets.

-Makes sense. You needed to learn about his operation.

-I followed my plan and bumped into Mister Muller on the street, the next day. I discretely expressed my interest in his latest project and he invited me to his house for a short discussion, over tea.

-What was his house like?

-It was dark, dusty, and full of books. From children's books to folklore books to George Orwell and Asimov, it seemed like Mister Muller was devouring all the literature he could get his hands on. He also followed the news closely and had a stack of newspapers on his desk, at all times.

-He had his finger on the pulse of society. Smart!

-Diabolically so. He gathered knowledge and was infamously able to twist it and use it to aid his rhetoric. You couldn't just dismiss him as a madman. He used dates, quotes, and statistics like no man I've ever met, before or since.

- What about the Overseer?

-The Overseer had no interest in using his vast knowledge to win debates. He never lied or twisted the facts. His knowledge came from the people themselves and was used to punish them directly, without mercy. The Dream Slayer, on the other hand, wanted to erase and replace what people believed to be true. He couldn't read minds but he wanted to enslave them instead.

-That sounds a lot more dangerous.

-It depends on your point of view, I suppose.

-So, did you get the book?

-After a grilling interview-like conversation, in which I had to prove my affiliation to Mister Muller's school of thought, he quietly handed me a small black booklet. It couldn't have been more than 80 pages. He called it his masterpiece, the crowning achievement of his work.

-The Sacred Order, right?

-Yes. He gave me three days to study it. I then had to return and discuss it with him.

-I'm really curious to learn what was in that book.

-I kept the copy to this day. If you wish, I can go and fetch it for you.

-No thanks. I'm not touching that with a ten-foot pole. Please, just summarize it for me instead.

-As you wish. The book had three pyramids drawn on its cover. They were stacked, forming a triangle with two on the base and one on top. Each pyramid represented a certain class of people and its proper place in the world. On the bottom left there was a red pyramid. It represented the working class, viewed by Muller as uneducated, crude, and easy to manipulate. In one word, they were a class born to serve. Next to it, on the right, there was a blue pyramid. It represented the businessmen, owners, bankers, and all the capitalists of the world. The money runners as Muller called them. He viewed them as no better than the crude workers. Their greed and general obsession with material possessions was a weakness to exploit, just as easily as the hunger of the humble worker.

-That's an interesting point of view.

-The bottom pyramids were therefore reserved to the slaves of the material world, those whose true freedom was taken away by that which they desire. The haves and have-nots were all equal in Muller's mind: Just a bunch of zombies fighting over a meaningless illusion. The millennia-old class war was the key, you see. The top pyramid was white. The color didn't represent any race or creed, however. It represented the Illuminated, those able to free themselves from the illusion of the physical reality, desiring nothing of it. Within this pyramid Muller placed all the good and evil in the world. To him, it was all the same. Those within the pyramid made the rules and designed the games for the bottom two pyramids to play.

-Why would they do that? For amusement?

-Not amusement but exaltation and transcendence. He viewed it as a form of divination, reading the mind of the Creator, thus becoming ever closer to him. The human experiment was theirs to conduct.

-But who sat at the top of that pyramid?

-That's the million-dollar question.

-It's those like Sassom and Urrud, isn't it?

-Muller never mentioned any aliens, conspiracies, or supernatural elements... Not once, in the entire book. He made a point of leaving that part up for debate.

-Or maybe he purposely wanted to confuse and create paranoia.

-As I was reading the book, I wondered: Which category do I fall in? Am I a slave or a philosopher-king perhaps? Am I both? Am I truly free? You see, Muller's genius was understanding the desire of people to view themselves as part of a hierarchy that had an invisible top of no particular creed. It made them accept the fact that all bets are off and the current order is just a game at best, and a meaningless illusion at worst.

-So, it was basically a kind of nihilist message disguised as something more profound?

-Not a nihilist message. Remember, he did mention the existence of an intelligent Creator. What he didn't mention is the location and nature of that Creator.

-I don't understand.

-Is the Creator separate from his creation? Is He good? These questions may sound silly, but they are the main themes of his work. He also never mentions God. He makes it clear that the Creator is not God, in the biblical sense. The Creator, our creator, has made some things but not all things. He, therefore, is a sort of "god" but not God almighty... That raises the question: Can anyone become a god, perhaps a living one? That is indeed a dangerous question to ask, in such a pyramid-based world, where some can freely play with the lives of others, and where good and evil are essentially the same thing.

-You believe it to be a perversion of the truth. You believe in absolute order and meaning, where everything is determined by that which lies above it. You believe that the same basic rules apply to everyone.

-I believe that this idea is what I'm fighting for. The monsters, however, are those who defy the natural laws. The Dream Slayer's weapon was just such a doctrine of defiance and corruption.

- But it served the purpose of his master perfectly.

-Exactly. I knew then that The Dream Slayer had to be eliminated, at all costs...

-But what if he was right, Victor? What if we are truly in a closed system, a game devised by some mad Creator who doesn't answer to anyone?

-You see how we are always tempted to accept such ideas as being valid? They divide us. They make some people feel like gods and they make others feel helpless and blind. They drag everyone away from the truth, from our true nature.

-It's what Urrud is counting on, isn't it?

-Maybe…

-So how did you do it?

-To put it quite simply, I burnt it all.

-Meaning?

-I quite literally burnt it all. On the third day, after completing my read, I decided not to return to Mister Muller's house. My hatred for him was too evident. He would have smelled it on me. Instead, I observed his house and realized he used his own basement as a printing press. He had all his equipment in there, plus a stash of books. He also used a small tool shed in the back yard for storage. I acted quickly, almost without thinking. At four in the morning, I jumped his fence, after using a small garden hose to pump out a few liters of gasoline form a car parked down the street. I quietly broke into the basement and soaked a room full of books and paper in fuel. I opened all the windows and threw a match inside. Then I quickly moved to the shed and lit it up. The whole place was up in flames, in a matter of minutes, since the old house had wooden floors and a wooden roof.

-But did Mister Muller burn as well?

-The house had two doors. I blocked the front door with a rusty bike chain and waited for Muller to exit through the back, where no one could see us. I had a shovel in my hand, borrowed from the shed. Minutes later, as the house turned into a huge bonfire, he busted through the door in flames. He immediately charged me, screaming and speaking in a language I didn't understand. His flesh was melting and falling off his blackened bones.

-Horrible!

-I jumped away and hit him in the back of the head with the shovel. That didn't stop him. I had to run around and hit him for five more minutes. After he finally collapsed, I had mere seconds to run away, before the police and firefighters arrived. By that time, there was nothing left of the house and Mister Muller. My own clothes had almost burned off and my face and hands were blackened by the smoke.

-Were there any suspicions of foul play?

-The fire brigade determined it was an accident, since the basement was full of flammable things and equipment. A faulty wire they said... But Mister Muller's followers didn't buy that. They scoured the streets in search of suspects for weeks. I had to keep my head down, since I had burns all over my hands.

-You were quite the efficient assassin, Victor. I would hate for you to come after me someday.

-I'm sure that won't be necessary, my dear.

-So, was that the end of it?

-Some of Muller's books were still out there, guarded by his acolytes, but since his untimely demise, they retreated into an obscure underground cult. You see, The Dream Slayer was the only connection between this army of lost souls and those friends he had in high places.

-The connection was now severed.

-The entire movement was halted. My little arson did sufficient damage. I didn't need to pursue the matter any further, at that time.

-At that time? Were there problems later? No, wait! Don't say it!

-We must part ways now, Madelyn. I want you to keep your eyes open and report any unusual things to me, when next we meet.

-Got it... My agent friend keeps calling me. I told him a little about you and he seems interested to meet. Just saying.

-We will decide how to come forward with this once I have completed relaying my story. Until then, keep those recordings safe and private.

-You don't need to worry, Victor. See you next week.

-Good bye, my dear.

CHAPTER 9

THE MIRROR MAKER

-Good afternoon, Madelyn. Please, come in!

-Hello, Victor.

-You look better. How are things going?

-Not much has improved, but at least I've been getting some sleep. I'm almost out of that wonderful tea, by the way.

-I'll have some more sent to you, later today.

-Thank you, that would be great. Do you know my address? It's...

-I don't need your address, my dear.

-What do you mean?

-When I send things, I don't exactly use a courier. I send them with Balthazar.

-Doesn't your man need my address?

-Balthazar is a raven and no, he doesn't need your address. He knows where you live.

-A raven? Are you serious? Wait, how does he know where I live?

-Balthazar is my eyes and ears out there. He knows many things.

-Including where I live. Did he... tell you?

-He shows me.

-In your mind? Like in that dragon show?

-Something like that.

-I don't believe that.

-You believe in monsters but you don't believe a raven could communicate with me?

-Where is old Balthazar now?

-Out there, searching for... something. You'll meet him soon enough.

-That sounds a bit creepy, Victor. Have you been watching me?

-I keep an eye on all my assets, as well as my friends.

-Yeah, well, next time just give me a call, like a normal person... Ha! What am I saying?

-I prefer my ravens if it's all the same to you.

-Don't know yet. Maybe Balthazar will convince me.

-You'll meet him soon enough, as I said.

-Can't wait...

-Shall we get to it, then?

-Sure, why not. Maybe I'll talk to Balthazar later, to see if he corroborates your stories.

-I see you're in a good mood today.

-Yeah, today wasn't complete shit, for a change.

-Then today is a perfect day to talk about the Mirror Maker.

-The Mirror Man? Sounds like an old artisan.

-That's exactly what he was, or appeared to be.

-Do you have any souvenirs from him?

-Actually, yes. The large mirror you see behind you was crafted by him.

-Wow! I've noticed that piece... Looks like an antique.

-18'Th century replica, silver on crystal, bronze frame.

-It's magnificent. How much does that even cost?

-Oh, it's not for sale, and even if it was, I have a feeling that you wouldn't want it anywhere near you... Not after you hear the story.

-I've always loved antiques, but I guess you're right... So, who was this Mirror Man anyway?

-He was an old craftsman. He owned a shop in the west of the city, well known and appreciated. In his shop, you could find all sorts of mirrors, from polished brass to black obsidian and even gold. He always fashioned his mirrors as inspired by his clients. The shop was full of them.

-Didn't he sell them?

-He did, but rarely accepted money for them. He usually bartered.

-Old fashioned indeed.

-The deals he made were extremely peculiar. I heard stories that made me think the matter was worth investigating.

-What sort of stories?

-Missing persons, persons who changed their behaviour overnight...Those sorts of things.

-So, what did you do?

-One morning, I went to the Mirror Maker's shop and asked for a commission. I was almost 16 by now and was big for my age.

-Didn't he sense who you were?

-He had me flagged from before I stepped across his threshold. A large black crystal mirror stood in the hallway of the shop. You couldn't see yourself in it but the Mirror Maker saw everything as soon as he looked in that mirror.

-Another mind reader, then?

-Not quite. The old man didn't see your thoughts, but he didn't care to see them. All he cared about was your aspect, your true shape.

-I don't think I understand.

-It's difficult to explain. He saw numerous dimensions of reality, beyond just space and time. He saw persons as nodes in a sort of eight-dimensional universe. He saw us as keys that can be used to influence the fabric of reality itself.

-That's harsh...

-He didn't care about our feelings or desires. Instead, he saw opportunities to sell us to his master for our true aspect, as he called it.

-The key aspect? I never saw people like that, until now. I don't think I'll be able to not think about this every time I meet somebody, from now on... Thanks for that.

-The Mirror Maker's way of seeing the world doesn't have to be your own, Madelyn.

-Yeah, but he was obviously on to something. I mean, Urrud doesn't waste his time with us just for fun, does he?

-The interesting thing is, Urrud wasn't behind the Mirror Maker's actions. The old man had a different master, one that was shrouded in mystery.

-Who?

-I don't know his name, but I got the feeling he was far older and more powerful than Urrud or Sassom.

-So, how do you know the Mirror Maker was a monster, then?

-Because of what happened next: As I sat there in his shop, staring at the many mirrors, I heard a voice coming from the walls themselves: "Have you come to fight me, young hunter?". The voice sounded almost condescending. I walked across the shop and entered the back room, where I saw a short but massive old man, carefully polishing a crystal mirror. His eyes were white and lifeless. When I asked him if he was blind, he replied that he didn't need eyes to see. The mirrors saw for him, more than I ever could. He then asked me to sit down, implying that he had an offer for me.

-He seems polite and even friendly.

-He then told me that I had an exceptional structure, one that can be used to access many doors. He wanted my help with opening just one of them. In exchange, he would fashion a mirror for me, one that would show me the way to achieve my greatest desires.

-Tempting, but what door did he need you to open?

-That's exactly what I wanted to know. He told me it was a door that would allow his master to search for his mother.

-That's it? Just search for someone? Seems sketchy.

-When I asked him about his master, he told me that his name could not be spoken there. He was too far removed from this world, too powerful. Naturally, I wondered why someone so powerful would need my help in locating his own mother, but who was I to judge? Those matters are still beyond my understanding.

-So, did you take the deal?

-I was hesitant at first, but it seemed like a harmless enough exchange. I didn't understand the motives but I felt like I didn't have to. Getting my own magic mirror sounded like a good bargain... In conclusion, I was to return to the shop the next week, to allow the Mirror Maker to complete his work. I had no idea what was waiting for me, upon my return...

-The monstrous part, I bet.

-Next Saturday I returned to the shop, as promised. The blinds were closed and I had to knock at the door insistently to be allowed inside. In the middle of the main room was a large round table and seated around it were six strangers. I counted three women and three men. They all had large mirrors positioned behind them, of various shapes and materials. Behind what was obviously my seat I saw the large elliptical mirror you've been admiring.

-Sounds like a perfectly creepy dinner party.

-Yes, only I didn't realise what was on the menu, until it was too late. The strangers all introduced themselves politely and sat back down, in silence. They acted like zombies, as if they were completely under the Mirror Maker's control.

-What about you? Were you also a puppet?

-I realized I was special in this particular group. Apart from being the youngest member, I was also the fourth male. I didn't feel compelled to act as I was told. I did it of my own free will. Later, I understood that my willingness was the key.

-So, if the others were on the menu, then you were desert.

-I was the last piece of a puzzle, one that was years in the making, perhaps even decades. The Mirror Maker was calm but you could sense he was excited to begin the ritual. The atmosphere was dark and gloomy... I just wanted to get it over with.

-What actually happened?

-The old man lit a single large candle and placed it in the middle of the table. He then closed all the lights and retreated into the darkness. All we could hear was his deep voice, which again seemed like it was coming from the walls around us. He began chanting in an unknown language. I found out it was probably old Sumerian, a language that was dead for thousands of years.

-Is that how old the Mirror Maker was?

-It is possible, yes. After minutes of dark chanting, I started to hear the screams of those around the table. One by one, they turned their faces towards the mirrors and became paralyzed with fear. The fear was so strong that they dropped dead where they sat, with a terrifying grimace still visible across their faces... Naturally, I was shocked and tried to get up but realized that I could hardly move. The Mirror Maker's hands rested on my shoulders, reaching from the darkness. "Sit down, Victor! It's almost over" he said, commandingly. In that moment I realized a terrifying truth: Behind me was the mirror and I heard no footsteps. The hands that reached out at me came from the mirror itself. The old man couldn't have been there.

-I hope you didn't turn around.

-I was tempted to, but seeing what happened to the others... I didn't dare do it. Soon, there was only silence. The voice of the Mirror Maker echoed across the room one final time: "I was right about you, Victor". Then, I saw the bodies being slowly dragged away into the darkness. A few moments later, the lights came back on and, to my surprise, everybody was gone. I was alone in the room and noticed that all the mirrors were cracked, except mine. Finally, the old man appeared, coming form the back room, and pointed towards the mirror. "It's all yours, Victor" he said happily.

-That was it? What happened to the others? Where did the bodies go?

-I didn't dare ask such questions, knowing that I would probably not like the answers, providing I could even understand them.

-You seem to have done well understanding monsters up to that point, even those as complex as the Dream Slayer. What made this Mirror Maker so hermetic?

-The fact that he didn't seem to care that much about our particular corner of the Universe, as Urrud did. He just used it as a sort of tool, if that makes sense. His didn't aim to torture, punish, or corrupt humans, but to use them and discard them. His motives were even further beyond my understanding, than those of the monsters I faced before him. I didn't even learn his master's name.

-You're not going to tell me more, are you?

-Some names cannot be spoken here, not truly.

-It's ok. I don't think I even want to know. Anyway, how did you kill the Mirror Maker?

-I didn't. Much like the Overseer, he was always two steps ahead of me, as blind as he was. Besides, he honoured our bargain and provided me with an important weapon for my arsenal. One that is precious to me, even now.

-What does that mirror do, exactly?

-For you or everyone else, it just does what all mirrors do. For me, it does a lot more. It reflects back pieces of the world, who are bound to me by desire.

-So it's like a compass for your soul.

-That's one way to look at it. Another is that it shows me the objects of my desire, as they truly are... Regardless, it is into that mirror that I looked one evening and saw the bloody sky turn into her hair and the earth turn into her skin. It is into that mirror that I saw the blood of innocents sinking into the abyss like an unstoppable whirlpool of corruption... And the abyss welcomed me as it turned into her eyes, her perfectly terrible eyes.

-The Red Girl...

-The one and only. The abomination that haunts my dreams and diminishes the light shining in my eyes, every waking moment of my existence.

-When did you see her next?

-Another time, my dear. Even talking about her depletes my soul of resources.

-Ok, Victor. I look forward to meeting Balthazar, later today.

-That you shall, my dear. Goodbye, for now.

CHAPTER 10

THE STONE GIANT

-Come in, Victor.

-Good evening, my dear.

-Tell me again why we're meeting in my office?

-The renovations at my home have reached quite the scale, I'm afraid. We would have no peace there.

-I see... Some of my colleagues seem a little freaked out by you.

-I don't blame them.

-You are elegantly dressed and all, but you do look like quite the eccentric gentleman.

-Is the cane a bit much for you?

-No, it's the rings.

-How so?

-I'm kidding. I guess people aren't used to your particular style.

-The cane, if you must know, was gifted to me by a very important person. It's both an accessory and a weapon. I never leave home without it.

-Can't you just get a gun like everyone else?

-Guns are too messy, too loud. I prefer swords and knives.

-I'm not going to argue with the expert. I just hope you never need to use them around me... Oh! Balthazar was delightful by the way. Such a wonderful bird!

-I'm glad you liked him.

-He knocked on my kitchen window then waited for me like a good boy. As soon as I opened he walked in and just placed the bag in my hand. Unbelievable!

-He's well disciplined.

-I even asked him if he would stick around for tea, if you can believe it. Imagine my surprise when he said ''no, thank you!'' in perfect English. I thought I was dreaming.

-He understands some words and can even formulate simple answers, but that's not how we communicate.

-You must teach me sometime.

-Perhaps. For now, I think we should continue with the story. This place makes me uncomfortable. It's too busy, too chaotic.

-As you wish, Victor. You know, my boss asked me why I was still interviewing you. I said I may actually publish your story.

-I see.

-Yeah… He started laughing hysterically. Funny thing is, when I asked him why he was laughing, he said that you wouldn't let me publish a single word. How would he know that?

-Frank always was a bit of an asshole, but a useful one.

-Wait! Wait! Wait! You two know each other?

-We go back a long time, actually.

-And why am I hearing about this now? Are you messing with me, Victor?

-Not at all, Madelyn.

-How do you know Frank O'Hara?

-Let's just say that twelve years ago, while I was on a hunt, Frank and his family got in the way. I had to save his ass before taking down a sinister stone giant.

-A wat? Ok, you have to tell me about this.

-Do I?

-Yes, Victor! Please!

-Maybe…

-Oh my God! It just hit me…

-What did?

-Frank didn't assign me to you because he thought you were insane. He actually knows you're the real deal!

-Let's just say your boss owes me. He knew that going public with my story would be risky, to say the least, so he assigned you to it, as punishment.

-Nice! In case it all goes south, I would take the fall.

-Something like that. I did however get him to change his mind.

-That was you? Damn it!

-I knew you shouldn't be forced to write about something. When I realized what he did, I called him.

-But I stuck around anyway.

-Much to Frank's surprise, apparently.

-Makes me wonder who else you know, Victor?

-I know many people, my dear, but I don't feel like discussing my relationships right now.

-Oh, I see. You can tell me about monsters but you can't tell me if you know the mayor or some judge?

-I only met the mayor of New York once, if you must know. We did however have a very interesting conversation about some of his campaign contributors.

-Oh, really? I thought you weren't into politics, Victor. How about senators or governors? Know any of those?

-Quite a few, actually.

-That's interesting... See, that sounds like the kind of story I would love to write. How does a poor Romanian immigrant in his forties get to know half the politicians in the country? Sounds quite amazing!

-I sense some anger in your voice, my dear.

-No shit! We've been talking about fairy tales for two months now, and it turns out you're some kind of shadowy kingpin to the political scene.

-I just steer people in the right direction, my dear. Nothing more. As I said, I don't like politics. My interventions amount to a bare minimum and not for the reasons you may suspect.

-Oh, that's what they all say, Victor. Until you find out they bribe and bully their way to getting some law or regulation pushed through, to make themselves filthy rich.

-I'm not interested in money, as you may have realized by now.

-Oh, I don't know. Your house looks like it costs a few cool millions and all your stuff doesn't exactly look cheap. Care to comment?

-When I first came to this country 15 years ago, I didn't come as a poor immigrant, my dear. I had made my fortune elsewhere. But that's a story for another time, perhaps.

-I see... Well, I guess the joke's on me, then.

-How so?

-I thought we were really connecting, Victor. I thought you were honest with me.

-I never lied to you.

-That may be true, but you weren't exactly forthcoming with a lot of important information, it seems.

-That information wasn't relevant to our story, at least not until now.

-Is that why you're telling me now? It's becoming relevant?

-Well, we skipped a few years but yes, I guess so.

-Then it seems that I'm operating on a need to know basis here. That your style?

-I find it's easier not to burden people with more information than they need to know. I often has... adverse effects.

-Ok, then I give up. You either answer some questions or I'm out. I don't like being kept in the dark.

-Professional defect, I suppose.

-Ha! You're the one to talk!

-Keep your voice down, my dear. I think your colleagues are freaked out enough as it is.

-I'm sorry... You're right. Will you answer?

-Shoot.

-Ok, ok, so, first of all, do you own any businesses here, in the U.S.?

-I own a consultancy firm and a real-estate business. I work with the church and some private companies.

-Consultancy, you say? What kind?

-The kind that needs total discretion. The kind you don't talk about.

-I thought we were being honest here.

-We are, but I'm not going to violate my client's privacy just to satisfy your curiosity, Madelyn.

-Ok, I guess that's fair. I think I have a basic idea of what you do for them anyway.

-I take care of unusual problems, shall we say.

-I figured. No need for specifics right now... Next question: How rich are you, really?

-You'll have to talk to my accountant if you need the figures. I don't concern myself with those details.

-Wow! I see! That rich, eh?

-The money I make gets used properly Madelyn, I assure you. My investments are well planned.

-Could you maybe give me an example?

-Certainly. For instance, I own two apartment buildings uptown. I bought them to ensure cheap rents to small income families when I heard the previous owners were planning on remodeling and kicking everyone out.

-That does seem genuinely impressive.

-I'm no saint, I assure you.

-No, I meant the fact that you could simply buy two buildings in uptown Manhattan. Who does that?

-I do. And believe me, the purchases were not without problems.

-I'm sure.

-I had altercations with many organized crime factions, with interests in the area. Some of them were even using my apartments to conduct drug deals.

-What did you do about them? I assume you didn't call the cops like everyone else.

-They tried to intimidate me.

-Ha-ha! I bet that didn't work out too well for them.

-No, it didn't. Some of them are still recovering, both mentally and physically. But we digress.

-No, I don't think so. Do you have many business associates?

-Some.

-May I know about them? What kind of people hang around Victor Rotaru?

-Two kinds: Those who consider themselves dammed and those who consider themselves privileged.

-Which category do I fall in?

-That's for you to decide.

-I see. Victor Rotaru is no shepherd. He's a one-man-army who gets things done. Whoever wants to hang around may do so at their own risk.

-Close, but not quite. I have taken a few apprentices over the years. I consider it my duty as a Touched, to find others like me and help them along their own path.

-Ok then, one last question: Why me?

-I'm not sure I understand.

-Why did you choose me to confide in, to share all this. It's clear that you did. You don't seem like the kind of guy who does anything by accident.

-You are very perceptive, Madelyn. That's what I like about you. You are also the essence of everything I'm not, not anymore I mean. You are so very... human. You are smart, dedicated, hardworking, and rational.

-I am the embodiment of your target audience, you mean.

-Close, but that's not all. If I can get you to open your eyes and see beyond the bricks and concrete, beyond papers and politics, the things you consider so tangible and real, then perhaps there is still hope.

-And how is that going?

-I'm not sure yet.

-About?

-About the normal person's ability to digest and deal with the things I deal with.

-Maybe Frank O'Hara was right when he said you wouldn't let me publish a single word.

-Perhaps, but perhaps not.

-I've been meaning to ask: What was all that about a stone giant? That seems outlandish, even by your standards.

-And so it was, even by my standards.

-Care to share?

-I don't see why not.

-Go on then! I'm listening. What exactly happened 12 years ago?

-Yellowstone Park, late September. Frank and his girls were hiking on one of the less popular trails. It started raining that afternoon. The ground became soft and muddy. The O'Haras took shelter under a large pine tree... That's where I first saw them.

-I didn't know Frank was an outdoor person.

-There's a lot you don't know about Frank, my dear. That day, he was more than prepared for a difficult hike, but he couldn't foresee what was about to go down.

-What about this stone giant? What kind of monster was it?

-I had been hunting the giant for a couple of weeks. He was extremely elusive and dangerous.

-How can a giant be elusive? I mean...

-He wasn't just a big brute. His ancient body was fused with a rare type of translucent white agate.

-What is that?

-Agate is a variety of quartz. It's a tough stone. Arrows and even bullets bounce off it, providing it's thick enough. Utu's stone shell was a foot thick.

-Jesus! How do you even kill that thing?

-That was my question as well. Of course, I would have to find him first. Utu would only come out at night or during the rain, never in the sun.

-That's curious.

-Not at all. Utu's semi-transparent shell offered him some interesting camouflage capabilities. It would borrow the ambient properties of his environment, changing color and brightness. However, under direct sunlight, the glare would expose him immediately.

-But it was raining that day.

-Yes it was. Frank chose the wrong place and time to take a stroll through the woods.

-So, this Utu, why was he a monster? What did he do?

-As I said, Utu was beyond ancient. These giants have been around since before mankind started documenting history. They are the stuff of legends and folklore, lost in the mist of time. However, this particular giant may have been the last of his kind. He always moved from place to place, never staying for more than a few weeks. Unfortunately, Urrud's corruption consumed him long ago.

-Wait, how big was this guy?

-About ten feet tall, maybe a bit more.

-So, how would a ten feet tall giant go about traveling around the world these days? I imagine he's not allowed on flights because of the weight issues.

-Utu always moved underground or underwater. I never fully understood how, but I suspect he was using a long-forgotten network of ancient tunnels.

-So, this guy could breathe underwater?

-Utu had become a sort of golem. He wasn't alive anymore, in the literal sense. His body was animated by Urrud's twisted energies.

-But what did he do exactly, when he reached one of his destinations?

-Utu was always searching for innocents. He used brutal, senseless murder to corrupt them.

-How could he corrupt them if he murdered them?

-Not them, but those they loved. You see, he had the appearance of a demon. When Utu came for those you loved, you would experience hell itself rise up and slaughter them with extreme prejudice. He would make you believe there is no earthly justice. He would make you believe that you are dammed... Eyewitnesses didn't dare report what truly happened, and those who did were ridiculed and even investigated.

-But weren't there signs and clues? Didn't the police find anything?

-Utu hunted in remote areas, not in cities. As large as he was, he was always careful not to leave any traces of his presence behind. He hibernated underground until he sensed an opportunity to strike... That day, in the forest, he had his eyes set on Frank and Melinda. Had I not intervened, he would have crushed them with a tree trunk in front of the girls, making it look like an accident.

-How exactly did you save them?

-I had a trap prepared for Utu. A huge pit filled with diesel fuel and wood, covered with leaves and sticks. Took me the better part of a week to set that up.

-You really enjoy burning things, I see.

-I find it's one of the best ways to eliminate monsters, without leaving much evidence behind.

-So, what happened?

-When Utu was nearby, I calmly approached the O'Haras. I was dressed as a park ranger to avoid any suspicions for lurking around so much. I told them that the trail was closed and dangerous because a mother bear and her cubs were spotted nearby. Minutes later, we were up on a ledge where I pretended to communicate our position by radio. I was actually talking to one of my assistants.

-You had assistants?

-I started paying people to help me with various tasks decades ago. Doing all the labor myself just wasn't practical. They didn't know much and I was careful not to create unneeded tensions.

-Ok. Am I one of your assistants now? Because I haven't received my paycheck yet.

-I pay cash.

-Oh, you got jokes now.

-Anyway, back to the story: After I got the O'Haras to the relative safety of that ledge, we all saw Utu burst through the trees, dragging a large pine trunk. He stopped below us and started hitting the rock wall, causing a rockslide. I turned to Frank and asked him if he wanted to get his family out of there alive. There was no way for me to protect them and we couldn't outrun a giant.

-Poor Frank must have been terrified.

-He didn't have time to be terrified. He did as I asked, to save those he loved. We climbed down and led Utu away from the women and into my trap. We ran as fast as we physically could, but the abomination was gaining on us. I told Frank to make a sharp turn just as we reached the covered pit. We barely made it... The monster was just a few feet behind us. His massive body didn't allow him to turn as fast as we did, so he stepped into the pit and fell with a terrible scream. The impact was so powerful that we felt the earth below us shake. As luck would have it, I dropped my lighter and my gasoline-soaked rag while running. Frank was our saving grace that day. I figured we had just moments before Utu would climb out of that pit and maul us to death.

-He smoked back then. He used to talk about giving up on a single day but never said how.

-I remember that Zippo as if it were in my hands right now. It had a wolf on the side, fangs out. I threw it in, praying to all the gods that it would stay lit and start the fire... We both watched it drop down in slow motion. When it hit the diesel-soaked leaves, nothing happened for a few seconds... Probably some of the longer seconds of my life. Utu was collapsing the walls around him fast, covering the wood with dirt. But soon the blaze started... In just under a minute, the flames got so high that we literally couldn't sit anywhere near that pit. We watched in silence from twenty yards away, hoping the giant wouldn't manage to jump out, somehow... We heard screams that no human ears have heard, before or since. The sounds almost turned me to stone, and I was already a seasoned hunter. I can only imagine what poor Frank felt.

-Holly God! I didn't know Frank went through all that. How the hell did he remain sane?

-As you can imagine, he and his family were in shock. I told him never to speak about this to anyone, or he would be in big trouble. He simply asked: "Talk about what?"

-He got the picture.

-I told him I would contact him someday, if I needed to. He made it clear that he owes me more than his life.

-Frank always pays his debts. That I know.

-Indeed he does.

-So, that leads us back here, to me.

-Now you know.

-Jesus! What was Frank even thinking? Does he want this out?

-I don't think he wants anything to do with it, but he probably wants something done.

-I guess it's up to you, then.

-It's up to us, my dear.

-I'm your co-conspirator now?

-Not just a mere associate after all.

-I'm flattered, but I don't know what to say at this point.

-That is indeed the appropriate response. Well, I have to leave you now.

-Ok, Victor. You've given me much to think about. See you next week.

-Stay safe, Madelyn.

CHAPTER 11

A MONSTER TO END ALL MONSTERS

-Hello Victor. How are the renovations going?

-Good afternoon, my dear. The renovations are on schedule. We should be finished by next week.

- I prefer meeting at your place. I don't like all the prying eyes here. They asked me about you, you know.

- I hope that wasn't too much of a bother.

-I just told them you were my crazy uncle from out of town.

-Crazy?

-Well, you have to admit, it's the simplest explanation.

-Yes, if only the simplest explanation were the right one, every time.

-Well, Victor, I know you're not crazy, if it makes you feel any better.

-I'm not entirely sure that's accurate but thank you, my dear.

-Ha! I guess we're all a bit crazy. I, for instance, have started seeing things.

-What kind of things.

-Ghosts in black robes flying through the sky, if you can imagine. It only happens when I'm tired, though.

-Hmmm... Ghosts you say?

-Yes, they're never aggressive. They just sit there, watching. Sometimes I hear them whisper.

-What do they say?

-They call me, they ask me to join them.

-I see... Do they frighten you?

-That's the strange thing. I don't feel frightened when I see them. I know I should be because they look terrifying.

-No matter, we will sort all of this out next week.

-What happens next week?

-You have to trust me, Madelyn.

- I do. You know, for the first time in my life, I truly feel as though I am part of something bigger, something important. It's a good feeling, Victor, no matter how strange this all is.

-I certainly understand that. The Creator has big plans for us all.

-I hope you're right. I hope there's something out there that makes all of this worthwhile. Something worth fighting for.

-There is, assure you.

-Tell me about her, Victor... Tell me about the Red Girl.

-To me, she's simply the monster to end all monsters.

-How so?

-Banishing her would mean ridding the world of Urrud's corrupted horde.

-But there are other monsters out there.

-There are, but something tells me that winning this fight would be a warning to them all.

-A warning?

-A warning that the human race is not weak or damned. A warning that we will fight back and protect ourselves. That is indeed a big part of my message.

-You want people to understand that? But how, Victor?

-There is a way to make them all see. For now, we will have to continue with our work.

-All right, Victor. What happened with that mirror of yours? Did it help you get to her?

-It did, but not in a way I was expecting it to.

-What did it show you?

-The Swiss Alps.

-What?

-It showed me that I needed to take a trip there, so I did. It took me all spring to convince my adoptive parents, but they finally agreed.

-What happened there?

-It was the summer of '94, I think. I was 17 and happy to be a normal teenager, for once. I even had a girlfriend whom my parents fully approved of. Her name was Greta.

-From school?

-She attended the same high school, even got better grades.

-Which I assume was saying something.

-I was certainly one of the best students in my class. I learned effortlessly.

-What about Greta?

-She was a bit of a genius herself, though she did spend a lot more time studying. My parents liked that.

-Yeah, because she didn't hang around all the time.

-That summer, they let her spend the vacation with me, her parents.

-Please tell me you didn't get the poor girl killed, Victor…

-Anyway, my teenage arrogance played a large part in convincing myself that I could handle my business and protect those I cared about.

-What happened?

-We were staying at this wonderful little hotel, up in the mountains. One night, while everyone was asleep, I felt a sinister and familiar energy, but I couldn't quite identify it. I grabbed a flashlight and decided to take a walk through the woods.

-A walk through the woods, alone, at night, in the mountains. What could possibly go wrong?

-That night there was a heavy mist out, blanketing the ground. At first, I could make my way through and kept my sense of direction. But soon, the lights of the hotel faded into the distance and I found myself surrounded by nothing more than dark pine trees. The mist had risen above my head. I couldn't see anything. But I still had my inner compass and decided to keep going.

-That sounds like a dumb thing to do, Victor, even for you.

-You must remember, this wasn't my first hike through the woods. I was quite experienced in this sort of environment. I had no fear of it.

-Something tells me that changed.

-After a few more minutes of walking, of following the dark energies, I heard screams echoing through the night. At first, I couldn't tell who it was but soon I realized it was Greta... She sounded terrified. The screams got louder and closer. I started running through the mist towards what I perceived to be the source, but the source kept moving, as if someone had grabbed poor Greta and was dragging her in circles around me.

-While you were running towards them? That hardly seems possible.

-Suddenly, I hit a large rock and tripped, hitting my head. Everything went dark. When I opened my eyes, I didn't know if minutes had passed or hours. Standing up, I realized something terrifying: I had lost my bearings. For the first time in my life, I was physically lost. I searched the ground around me for the flashlight but couldn't find it. It was pitch black. I could hardly see the shape of the trees that were just inches in front of my eyes. I screamed for Greta but there was no answer... The darkness swallowed my words whole as soon as I spoke them, like a hungry beast. Soon, an eerie silence filled the air, chilling me to the bone. I felt the dark energies amplify. Even the voices of the spirits that were usually accompanying me were silent, as if they had been scared off by some sinister presence. I felt a great terror fill my soul, knowing that I was truly helpless and alone. My trusty knife was still at my side but offered me little comfort against the endless night.

-Jesus! I think I would have died that night... How did you get out?

-After what seemed like hours of shambling through the darkness, I saw a small flickering light through the trees. Surely it was the hotel, I thought to myself. I started walking towards it as fast as I could, hitting branches and tree trunks in the process. I felt warm blood gushing out of my face and hands, but desperation kept me going. As I approached, the light became brighter and slowly changed color, from yellow to red...

-It was her, wasn't it?

-At first, the red was bright but soon turned into a dark crimson. The more I approached, the more it felt like it wasn't even there. The last few steps I took towards it were mostly out of some misplaced inertia of hope. I realized the light was no light at all, but long crimson-red hair... Then, she whispered my name in an unnatural voice, not the childish voice I remembered.

-How, Victor? How did you survive?

-I'm not sure I did, not entirely anyway. The girl I knew before wasn't there. As terrifying as the Red Girl was to my seven-year-old self, I could never have imagined the horror that stood before me... The abomination was flickering in and out of sight, moving around me, toying with my senses. When she finally stopped, she stood just three steps away from my face.

-Can you describe her?

-She was tall and slim, wearing a torn white silk gown that was long beyond reason. Sheets of white silk floated in the cool wind and twisted around nearby trees, appearing alive. Her face was darker than the night itself. Only a pair of terrible yellow eyes pierced through a motionless façade. Her long ghost-white arms opened as if waiting for my embrace. The silence broke with a single ice-cold sentence: "I have missed you, little Victor".

-And then you ran the hell out of there and survived, right?

-I grabbed the knife but I felt my strength failing me. She got to me like no monster ever could... I knew I couldn't kill her. I knew she would use all my strength against me, like before. It felt like hours had passed before she broke the silence again: "I have a gift for you, little Victor. Follow me."

-And, naturally, you did. You followed your biggest foe into the night...

-There was no choice, Madelyn. I was unprepared and quite helpless against her. Besides, our bond, as twisted as it may have been, was quite unbreakable. My tortured soul required answers only she could provide.

-Where did you go?

-We walked up to a large boulder. The Red Girl floated above it and presented me with a choice: Either dig up what was under the boulder and keep it, or be killed where I stood.

-Since you are here, I assume you took the first option. What was under that boulder, Victor?

-I started digging with my bare hands, drenching the earth in blood. Minutes later, I unearthed a large metal chest. Inside it were large gold bars, much to my surprise. Over 300 kilograms in total, as I later found out.

-What? So, either take the gold or get killed? That doesn't sound like a hard choice at all.

-I remember picking up one of the bars. It was ice-cold and extremely heavy. The pale yellow light pouring out of the abomination's eyes was sufficient for me to make out a swastika and some writing.

-Oh...

-The Red Girl told me that 72 children had stained that gold with their blood. It belonged to a Nazi doctor who did... unspeakable things.

-So, you just took it?

-I had to accept a fortune acquired with innocent blood, and I had to spend every cent of it myself. The blood pouring out of my cuts stained the gold bar and made me understand: I was falling even deeper into the abyss that Urrud had prepared for me. But the choice was simple: either accept or die.

-Couldn't you just... leave it all there? I mean, ok, it was yours, but couldn't you just leave it alone?

-That's not the way this works, Madelyn. A deal made with Urrud is not a contract you can just get out of. His promise to leave humanity to its own devices, should I succeed in banishing the Red Girl, would no longer have been valid. You see, each new contract was based upon the last... Still, I suppose I could have left the gold there, untouched, but I could never have achieved the things I have... You and I would have never met.

-You thought you could cheat Urrud by putting the gold to good use?

-Not cheat, but at least diminish my shame. The mirror had led me to what I desired but also needed. It had somehow changed my fate.

-The mirror forced Urrud to give you millions in gold?

-Perhaps. The forces at play were unclear to me. They partly remain so, to this day. One thing is for sure: I walked out of that forest the next morning, alive and dragging a jacket stuffed with gold bars.

-Sure sounds like a miracle.

-The whole thing changed me. It showed me that I was prepared to overlook things, important things, in order to get things done. It showed me just how thin the grey line between light and darkness can be, sometimes.

- We all walk that thin line at some point, Victor.

-We do, especially when the only other option is death.

-But you made the best of it, didn't you?

-I tried to, for me and for her.

-Her?

-Greta...

-Victor?

-She wasn't in the room when I returned. The police found her in the forest, mauled to death by what seemed to be a bear. I was the only one who knew what truly happened that night but I never shared it with a single soul, until today.

-Jesus! Poor girl!

-Her death made me realize two things: That I would be forever reminded of my weakness and that I would always remain alone. I could never protect the ones I cared about from Urrud's army. That day, at 17, I resigned myself to a life of loneliness.

-Victor...

-It's quite all right, my dear. As it turns out, loneliness has its own benefits.

-No one should walk through life alone, Victor.

-Yet some of us do. It all is as it should be.

-But if anyone can change their destiny, it's you... You can defeat her. You can step out of the shadows.

-That's kind of you to say, Madelyn, but I'm not sure that's possible, even for me.

-The monster to end all monsters indeed... Well, I believe in you, Victor.

-That belief may be soon tested. Until then, I leave you to enjoy the rest of your day in peace.

-Ok, Victor. See you next week.

-My house, this time. Good afternoon, my dear.

CHAPTER 12

THE BLUE BARON

-Hello, Victor! What was the urgency? ...Wow! This place looks different.

-Good afternoon, Madelyn. Yes, as I said, I got rid of all useless artifacts and memorabilia.

-I never figured you for a minimalist, Victor.

-It is a matter of necessity.

-How so?

-It's difficult to explain at the moment. Please, come this way.

-I see the mirror is still here. You couldn't get rid of it.

-No, I still need it. Please, let's begin.

-Ok. Why the rush?

-There isn't much time, I'm afraid. Follow me, I need to show you something.

-You never did take me on a tour of your house. This should be interesting.

-Not as interesting as it was before, I assure you.

-Yes, but I guess we never did have time for that. Oh, by the way, I won't be able to make our next meeting. I'm going to Boston for a week, to see my mother.

-Is that so?

-Yes, we don't talk much lately... I was thinking of surprising her with a visit.

-That's very good of you, dear.

-So, where are we going?

-Right through here! Watch your step.

-What is this place? What's that on the walls?

-Silver.

-It's so well polished! I can see my reflection in the slabs, just like in a mirror. Victor, this must have cost a fortune.

-No expenses were spared.

-And the floors! Wow! That deep blue is simply amazing.

-It's Afghan Lapis Lazuli.

-Jesus! I don't even want to know how expensive that was.

-Lapis was considered by the ancients to be a stone of wisdom and truth. It amplifies psychic energies, making you see things clearly... I also find it calms the spirits.

-It calms me too. The colors are simply amazing.

-I'm glad you like it.

-What is this all for, Victor? I'm sure you didn't spend a fortune just to make a pretty room. And what is behind that creepy metal door?

-So many questions! To answer them, we have to go back in time and share a little story.

-Can I sit here?

-Please.

-These chairs are fantastic.

-Romanian oak, the very best.

-Ok then, I'm waiting for all this to make sense.

-Fifteen years ago, I came to this country following a lead. I believed it was the one thing that could finally give me an advantage in my struggles.

-What kind of lead?

-A man, Romanian. He came here a few years after the Romanian Revolution. His name was Dan Rosca. I tracked him all the way back to the village I lived in, with the priest's family.

-Who was he?

-He couldn't have been more than five or six years older than me. He was the son of Anton and Lucia Rosca, a couple of farmers whose youngest daughter vanished in mysterious circumstances. The girl's name was Ileana Rosca...

-Ileana? Wait, Ileana, where have I heard that name before? The old woman back in the village, wasn't her granddaughter's name Ileana? Wasn't Ileana actually...

-The Red Girl, yes.

-So, this guy, Dan, he was the Red Girl's actual brother?

-Indeed he was. As it turns out, he was quite the monster himself. Urrud got to him when he was just a young boy, devastated by his sister's disappearance... and a whole lot of other things.

-Jesus! And this guy came to the US?

-He did, probably around '92 or 93'. He couldn't have been more than 22 back then, but was already quite the beast. He quickly made a name for himself, doing despicable things like child trafficking and pornography. You see, there was no shortage of orphans in Romania, back then. Dan helped set up so-called "adoption networks".

-This is disturbing, Victor.

-By the time I got to him, he built a whole empire on secrets and blackmail. He had judges, bankers, and politicians in his pocket... A ring of "elites" who were actually a group of ruthless, disturbed pedophiles.

-I hope you killed that sick son of a bitch.

-This... creature was so vile, that he even let his own daughter be taken advantage of, by one of his clients.

-Daughter?

-Yes, he married, to keep up appearances. But his family was no more than a cover story to him, just like his legal businesses, the pawnshops and antique stores.

-Victor...What...what are you saying?

-Life can sometimes be so cruel.

-My... my father's name was Daniel.

-I'm so very sorry, Madelyn...

-No, no, no! No! My dad's dame was not Rosca. This isn't right.

-I wish I could take all the pain away, my dear, I truly do.

-Stop it, Victor! This is madness!

-Did you know he called himself "the Blue Baron"? He even had those blue handkerchiefs engraved with a double "B" inside a triangle.

-Why... is this happening? God!

-You must have seen them when you were young, before he ...went away.

-Victor, what did you do?

-You must understand, Madelyn, he truly was a monster. But I think you already know that, don't you? I can only imagine what...

-Shut up! Shut up for a second! I... I need to go, right now.

-I don't think that's a wise thing to do, Madelyn. I think now, more than ever, you need to sit down and listen. Everything depends on it.

-No, I need to go. Leave me alone! I need to go and talk to my mom. She knows, she'll tell me the truth.

-You already know the truth. It's just a matter of time before you accept it. You buried this, Madelyn, for so many years. I don't expect you to be all right... I know it hurts.

-Shut up, you son of a bitch! What do you know? Tell me, Victor! Have you been planning this the whole time? Have you been stalking me, you sick bastard?

-I have been protecting you, as best I could.

-Protecting me from what? My dead father? What?!

-Please, sit down.

-I need to go right now. I... I need to go see mom.

-Madelyn, stop! Please!

-Leave me alone, Victor.

-You need to stop!

-No!

-Your mother is dead, Madelyn!

-Wha... what?

-She died last Friday... Urrud's slaves got to her.

-Where is she, Victor? How do you know this?

-Balthazar has seen it. I'm terribly sorry, my dear, but you won't find her... She's quite simply... gone.

-You're lying! Do you want to destroy me? Why?

-She hasn't been answering your calls, has she?

-She's... busy.

-That's why you are going to see her, isn't it? You are worried.

-Get out of my way, Victor!

-Madelyn, if you go out that door, I can't protect you anymore. Do you understand that?

-Protect me from what? What are you talking about?

-I swore never to let anyone I cared about suffer because of me, because of the life I live. I can deal with loneliness, Madelyn, but I'm not sure I can handle any more guilt.

-You should've thought about that before you got my mother killed! You asshole!

-I couldn't save her, but I can save you. And you can save me, Madelyn. You can save us all!

-Get out of my way, Victor!

-If you leave, Urrud's pawns will have you killed before the next sunrise. Don't you get it? You and I, our fates are bound together now. There is no other way.

-I'll take my chances. Move!

-You are damning us all, Madelyn!

-So, now the fate of mankind rests solely on my shoulders? How? Why?

-The Red Girl is your aunt, she's your flesh and blood. Isn't it obvious?

-What? Just say it!

-You're the only one who can stop her. But we have to move fast, before Urrud's slaves find a way in here.

-They're coming here?

-For now, we are safe. Balthazar is watching over us.

-Why here? Why now? What's the urgency? Haven't you been hunting these abominations for decades?

-And they have been hunting as well.

-Hunting who?

-Your family, your bloodline. They need you gone... He needs you gone.

-Right, because I'm the only one who can stop... her. Right? This is ludicrous!

-This is the truth, Madelyn.

-But why now? What did you do, Victor?

-I will explain everything but please, sit down.

-Ok... but no more bullshit, Victor. No more riddles. Just straight up tell me.

-When I... ended your father, Urrud spoke to me and warned me that my actions would cost the lives of many innocents. He tried to place all the guilt on me.

-Well, it appears that both of my parents are dead because of you, so maybe you should feel fucking guilty!

-When I took down your father's empire, many of his... associates put a gun in their mouth or hanged themselves. They would rather die than face the consequences. They could not live with their actions.

-Good! A bunch of vile monsters!

-But it didn't just end there. Many others took steps to protect their power. They didn't want to be brought down because of your father's failures.

-What kind of steps?

-They made people disappear. People who could identify them. People who could testify. I'm talking secretaries, staff, lower-level members, and, worst of all, the victims. Those who survived were now hunted down. I couldn't stop it. I tired. There were just too many of them and just one of me... I consider it one of my greatest failures.

-Jesus! Couldn't you have gotten some help?

-These people, Madelyn, they aren't your average criminals. They control the system and everyone in it. They are themselves pawns of another group, one even more twisted than them.

-Who? What is this group that controls everything?

-There are things that even I dare not speak of, unless I wish to bring down heavy burdens upon those who learn the truth.

-I think we're past that point now, Victor.

-It's one thing to talk about the supernatural and unnatural, because they are subjects hardly tangible to everyday life. No one takes them seriously enough because no one sees the direct impact on their lives. It's just too abstract.

-Ok. I get that. These people are flesh and blood, though. They walk among us, right?

-That's what makes them so dangerous to the average people out there. They are predators who would stop at nothing to maintain and amplify their power.

-But how are they connected to Urrud?

-Urrud and Sassom are two of the puppeteers. I have yet to find the unnatural top of this dark pyramid.

-You have yet to tell me who these people are, the ones that are part of the pyramid.

-They go by many names, deliberately chosen to deceive you. They hide behind groups of interest and various organizations that they use as fronts and scapegoats, if the need arises. They have always been here, in one form or another, since ancient times... These monsters thrive on the misery and suffering of others, seeing people as nothing more than a kind of livestock.

-Yeah, I've heard it all before, the myths, the conspiracies. But no one seems to show me who ''they'' truly are... It appears that you can't either, or won't.

-I'm trying to protect you, Madelyn. I know that you would go out there like a good journalist and investigate, trying to expose them.

-Exactly! That's my job.

-You have no power, dear girl. Many powerful and highly influential people have died, trying to expose them.

-What about you, Victor? Do you have any power?

-My power, both natural and supernatural, is only effective because I have no ties, no real connections with the outside world. I have always been like this, and not by accident. It allows me to maneuver freely and unseen. The few associates I have are the kind of people who won't share my secrets.

-How so?

-I only work with the blind or deaf. I try to help them as much as they help me.

-But what can we do, Victor? Why are we here, now, in this weird, silver-plated, insanely expensive room? What is your plan, exactly?

-It all has to do with what's behind this one and a half ton steel door.

- And what's in there, Victor?

-I think you must know, by now.

-No, I don't.

-You must feel it. You, Madelyn, are not as ordinary as you think.

-Jesus! Is it... It can't be.

-Behind that door is the Red Girl. I have finally captured her, last Thursday.

-How? How is that possible?

-I think you need to rest now, my dear. There is much you need to think about. Grief for your mother, remember her... Don't worry, you are quite safe here.

-Can I stay?

-I'll show you to your room, upstairs. Come, we'll talk again later this evening, over dinner.

CHAPTER 13

THE BLOOD WARDEN

-Good evening, Madelyn. Did you sleep well?

-Not really.

-Please, sit down. Maria has prepared a traditional Romanian meal for us.

-This all looks delicious, Victor.

-Maria is quite the cook.

-Look, Victor, I have to say something. I know I freaked out back there but you have to understand, all of this is really hard to process... I'm sorry and thank you for watching over me, all this time.

-No apologies needed, my dear. I have to say, you're actually handling this a lot better than I thought.

-Well, you did prepare me for a couple of months... Still, that last part was a hard punch.

-I do regret my blunt approach, but I'm afraid the urgency demanded it.

-I just keep thinking about mother... I hope she didn't suffer.

-I'm truly sorry... If it's any consolation, she passed quickly and without pain.

-How... how do you know this?

-When the Blood Warden comes for you, you usually don't see him coming. You're just... gone.

-The Blood Warden?

-Urrud's champion... A horror like no other.

-Who is this monster?

-He's an assassin, a damned efficient one. I've never been able to end him, all these years. In fact, he almost killed me twice.

-Jesus! Can you even stop him?

-In theory, yes. But he is faster and stronger than me… His skill with blades is unlike anything I have ever encountered.

-And he…

-It was him, yes.

-But if you knew my mother was in danger, why didn't you warn her, or me?

-You and your mother only became targets after I captured Ileana in Italy, last Thursday. The hunt was a longshot, to be honest. I didn't expect to succeed and I didn't expect Urrud to act so quickly. Your mom… she was dead before I even returned to the US. I don't understand it.

-Understand what?

-How the Blood Warden found her so quickly. I thought that if she managed to stay hidden and safe all this time…

-That one more day wouldn't be a problem? I get it. You know, I never understood why she moved to Boston and married that douchebag Anthony, after father disappeared. I guess it all makes sense now.

-She needed to hide. A guy who owned a private security company was a good bet.

-Owned?

-Urrud's champion got them both, along with two of Anthony's men. The official story is that they are missing. The truth is that the Warden consumed them, leaving no trace. That's what he does.

-Jesus! Why didn't the police call me? And how am I still alive?

-The police know the Warden's handy work well. They probably filed in missing person reports like so many times before and... forgot to inform you.

-Forgot?

-Boston PD detectives know not to get involved. If Urrud's assassin is hunting, they don't need to inform the potential victims, unless they want to become victims themselves. How you managed to remain alive for three days is beyond me, if the Warden found your mother.

-Perhaps he needs me alive. Perhaps Urrud has other plans for me.

- Your family can channel great power for him, as Ileana has proven. The Warden may attempt to capture you at this time, killing me in the process.

-How long has this been going on, Victor?

-The Blood Warden has been taking care of the Order's problems for decades. He's also the reason Urrud manages to control them so well.

-Is this "Order" the one we're not talking about?

-The Order that shall remain nameless, for now.

-Not really nameless if we're calling it something.

-Anyway, we should start preparing. There isn't much time.

-Much time before what?

-Before the Blood Warden himself knocks on our door.

-I'm scared, Victor... But you know what? If this asshole needs me alive, perhaps we can use that.

-Yes... we could set a trap for him.

-If this Blood Warden is Urrud's champion, the key to his power here, then we need to take the son of a bitch down.

-A task I haven't been able to accomplish so far... We need to think strategically, Madelyn. Remember, we have the Red Girl. If we destroy her, then Urrud will withdraw from this world forever, as promised.

-Do you really believe he'd actually do that?

-Without a doubt. Urrud is a corruptor, not a deceiver. He will live and die by his word.

-That's unbelievable. I don't understand why a demon as evil as he is would actually honor his word.

-As I've said, Madelyn, I'm not sure what Urrud is. Perhaps we will never find out.

-Well, if we ever will, then we have to act now.

-I agree.

-What's the plan?

-If I am correct, we only have a few hours before the Blood Warden manages to break in here. We need to use that time wisely.

-Wait, what's stopping him from marching in here right now?

-His memories.

-His what?

-The reason I have been able to stay alive for so long is that I always do my homework... Before becoming Urrud's champion, the Black Warden was a devout catholic, a member of the Opus Dei... His name was Ignacio Sanchez. As the years passed, his devoutness was turned into fanaticism by one of Urrud's pawns, a sinister Jesuit priest.

-The Opus Dei? Jesuits? Victor, what is this?

-We don't have time for details, Madelyn. The Jesuits used Ignacio to solve various problems with members who had caught the spotlight for the wrong reasons.

-You mean child molesters.

-Ignacio did his duty, spilling the blood of those who would threaten the church's image. He was called upon to deal with recent cases, those for which the statute of limitations would not prevent legal proceedings against members of the clergy.

-Yeah, I covered some of these stories. The recent ones always seem to hit a dead end.

131

-Quite literally dead, in some cases. Anyway, Ignacio's corruption by Urrud became stronger, overwhelming his body and soul. But the memories of his deeds would always haunt him.

-How does this help us?

-As you know, I have quite the gift when it comes to communing with the dead... There is no shortage of restless spirits, seeking retribution for Ignacio's crimes. These spirits act as my guardians against him. So far, he has never managed to get to me.

-Something tells me that won't stop him tonight.

-Perhaps not, but it will give us an advantage, since Urrud is desperate to retrieve the Red Girl before we dispose of her.

-The Warden will be forced to intervene, in spite of our home turf advantage.

-Precisely. That, and the fact that he needs you alive, may just give us the edge in this fight...

-How do we kill her, Victor?

-The Red Girl cannot be killed by any violent means. I have tried and failed, many times. She feeds on violence and anger. You, however, may have a chance.

-How?

-Your blood is literally poisonous to her. You see, no blood flows through her veins anymore. It has long been replaced by a black ooze of corruption. Her blood is an abomination and yours is the means to cleanse it, since it was once her own.

-You want to... feed the monster my blood?

-That's the problem. She will sense any attempt to deceive her. She will only feed on your blood if...

-Say it, Victor.

-If she believes we mean to hurt her some other way.

-You mean if we go in there and attack her, then, when she fights back, you let her feed on my blood?

-I'm afraid that is the only way.

-Wait, can't we just transfuse the blood, somehow?

-We don't have time for that. I don't have the means to restrain her anymore. That was a one-off kind of deal.

-Didn't you once say that wood hurts her?

-It used to. Now, only Romanian oak has any effect, a very limited effect. That's how I got her here.

-Then, I propose we make some wooden stakes and we use my blood on them.

-That... may actually work. It may not kill her but it will damage her enough to allow us a chance at injecting her.

-Ok then. It's definitely better than feeding me to her.

-Come, quickly!

-Where are we going?

-...Here, use these syringes.

-All of them?

-Tie this around your arm, tight. I'll do the rest.

-There... hurry up before I change my mind.

-Ok. Stay still.

-Ah! Careful!

-I regret that my nursing skills aren't fully developed.

-To say the least...

-That's one... Hand me another!

-Here you go... I'm scared, Victor.

-Don't worry, please! As I said, I'll do the rest.

-The hell you are! I'm going in there with you.

-Madelyn, you don't have to. I can handle it.

-Listen to me! If there's even a small chance that this doesn't work, then we're fucked. She'll be on to us, with the blood I mean. We won't get a second chance. If I'm in there, then...

-It won't come to that.

-It better not, but can you guarantee it?

-I cannot guarantee anything.

-You said it yourself, we don't have much time… Victor?

-No, we have no time…

-Victor?

-He's here.

-Fuck! Hurry up with that blood!

-That's five. I hope to God that's enough.

-Lead the way!

-He's fighting the spirits. We go in now, with all we have. The steel door will stop him.

-I'm scared as fuck, Victor.

-No, Madelyn, you are the bravest woman I have ever met… Go! Down these stairs!

-What are those screams?

-It's Ignacio. He's in pain… He's coming.

-Shit!

-Listen to me carefully, Madelyn. Behind that door is a horror like you've never seen before, not even in movies. She's going to shock you. You will feel weak and paralyzed. You have to fight her, you have to dig deep. We only get one shot at this, so shut down your emotions and focus. The tip of this spear and her chest are the only things in the world you need to see… Do you understand me?

-Victor, I'm… I'm ready. I'm ready to die.

-I'm proud of you. No matter what happens, you need to know that.

-Thank you…

-Look at me! I go in first. We'll need to flank her then get her in the corner. No mercy!

-Ok, ok, ok. Open it! Open it now!

-Go!

-Shit!!! Holly God! What is that thing?

-Strike her! Strike her now!

-Ah! Fuck! I got her!

-In the corner! Keep stabbing her!

-The syringes! Go for it!

- Ahhh!

-Do it! Die, you fucking bitch!

-I injected her! Step back!

-What's happening? Why is she shaking like that?

-I don't know. Stay back and keep your spear up!

-She's down!

-Quickly, close the door! Close it now! Ignacio is here!

-He's right outside, Victor! I saw him. He's in your silver room!

-There! Give me the last one!

-Be careful!

-That's three syringes. Jesus, the needles almost broke in her skin! We won't be using them again.

-Should we keep stabbing her?

-The spears are blunted and the blood has dried. There's nothing more we can do. Hitting her now will actually feed her.

-Then this is it, Victor.

-This is it...

-She's not screaming anymore. She's not moving.

-Stay back! She's not dead yet.

-Jesus, Victor! Look at her... It's unthinkable.

-Go look through the glass. I'll keep an eye on her... Don't worry, that's bulletproof. Just shut the blinder back when you're done.

-He's there. He's literally sitting in your chair.

-Because he knows there's no way out of here, except through him...

-What happens now, Victor?

-There are only two ways this plays out... We either killed Ileana and the Warden backs out, bound by Urrud's words, or...
-Or?
-Or Ileana wakes up... And if she doesn't kill us in here, then the Warden will, out there.
-What if she just lies there in a coma? We'll starve in here!
-I'm afraid we'll die of thirst long before we starve.
-That's not helping... Holly fuck! Look at that sword! ...And he looks like he could chop me in half with one swing.
-Calm yourself. He's not trying to get in.
-Why is that? Isn't he afraid we're going to kill the Red Girl?
-We already played that card, I'm afraid. Short of force-feeding her pieces of you, there's nothing more we can do.
-But what is he doing?
-He's waiting.
-For what?
-He's waiting to see if we killed the Red Girl... It appears our situation has become a bit like Schrodinger's cat in a box.
-What?
-The physicist Erwin Schrodinger once proposed an interesting thought experiment, in order to better explain quantum uncertainty. He proposed that if we place a cat in a box containing a radioactive material that could randomly decay at any time, triggering a kill mechanism, then, from the outside, the cat would be alive and dead at the same time.
-What the fuck, Victor?
-You see, since the poison could randomly trigger at any time, there is no way of knowing if the cat is alive or dead, from the outside perspective. It could be dead in minutes or fine for a long time.
-Without food and water?

-That's not the point. The point is, from the outside, the cat is in a state of uncertainty. It's simultaneously alive and dead.
-Yeah, until you open the box and see for yourself.
-That's precisely my point!
-I don't get it...
-When you open the box, the uncertainty ends and you have an outcome.
-So?
-So, theoretically, we and Urrud live in two different worlds, until that door opens. Our world guarantees an outcome. His world doesn't.
-Holly God! I think I understand.
-Urrud's energies can't penetrate these walls. I made sure of that. But he does know we used your blood, which may or may not kill Ileana.
-So, for the outside world, the Red Girl is both alive and dead. For Urrud, it's game over and game on, at the same time...
-As long as this door is closed, Urrud's presence out there is haunted by this paradox.
-But he has a one in two chance of winning if the door opens. Those are pretty good odds.
-I'm not sure what the odds are, but Urrud doesn't gamble. That's not the way he functions.
-So, I guess that means it's our move.
-The problem is that time is against us.
-We're either going to get killed by her or by thirst. Fuck!
-Yes...
-The Blood Warden is literally using time against us.
-Urrud has probably calculated that there is a chance for us to make a desperate attempt to fight Ignacio and flee before Ileana's fate is determined in here. That would change everything.
-Why?

-Because, instead of taking the odds as they are, of your blood killing her, he would improve those odds in his favor. If we burst out of here while she still exists, then the Warden could revive her, possibly.

-But there's another possibility, Victor. What if we walk out of here after she dies? Wouldn't that mean he loses?

-It would indeed, but those are still the same odds as before. He has nothing to lose by waiting us out, but everything to gain.

-Are you sure he can't get in here?

-Not before we either die or open that door ourselves. The reinforced concrete walls are over three feet thick and that door can withstand explosive blasts. It would take him days to get in here, if he had heavy power tools. My guardian spirits will allow nothing of the sort... He's barely keeping them at bay as it is.

-Can't Urrud send others?

-He has no lesser pawns that could get anywhere near this place. I have called upon all my guardians.

-Ha! Then I guess that the dice have been cast.

-Indeed they have. There's no way we walk out that door before we see her dissolve into nothingness.

-Wouldn't that have happened by now?

-Not necessarily. I have seen poisons take days, even weeks to kill.

-Can he...

-Hear us? Not unless you open that hatch and speak loudly.

-Should we talk to him?

-Maybe later. For now, I think we should conserve our strength.

-By the way, you never told me what that room is for.

-You'll see... We may yet walk out of here alive.

CHAPTER 14

THE VAMPIRE

-Hey, Victor! Wake up!

-I'm awake. Just resting my eyes.

-It's your turn to keep watch.

-Any changes?

-Nope. She's still not moving. I think her hair...

-Yes?

-I think her hair is getting brighter. Maybe I'm just imagining it.

-No, I think you're right.

-What does that mean?

-She may be regressing to her human shape.

-Is that good or bad?

-I don't know yet... I have only seen this once.

-What happened?

-It was a vampire. He regressed to his mortal shape then died, poisoned by his own noxious blood.

-That's good news, right?

-Not necessarily. The Red Girl isn't a vampire. She may be using her lesser shape to neutralize your blood.

-Well, Fuck! When will we know?

-How long has it been?

-Let's see... It's four in the morning. We've been in here for almost eight hours.

-Not long enough.

-No shit! I don't know If I can stay down here much longer, Victor. That... thing is freaking me out.

-You get used to it.

-I don't want to get used to it. I want to get the fuck out of this bunker, alive.

-You and me both, but our duty still remains.

-By the way, Ignacio is starting to get agitated, out there.

-Yes, I imagine all those memories my guardians are forcing him to relive are quite agonizing.

-Good! Can they actually kill him?

-No, but they may eventually knock him out. We have to pay close attention. If they do, we may have seconds to finish him off.

-That's good to know...

-He's especially tormented out there, in that room.

-Yeah, you were going to tell me about that.

-That room was designed as a last-ditch defense mechanism against intruders.

-How does it work?

-Those of unnatural origin and tormented nature have a hard time staying in there. The silver mirrors reflect more than just their twisted image back. They also reflect destructive energies, giving them a taste of their own medicine. In addition, the Lapis Lazuli is meant to force them to face their true nature, to dwell on it.

-That must be torture to a beast like Ignacio.

-I'm counting on it.

-How long can he keep this up?

-I don't know, but let's pray it's not too long.

-Amin!

-Twelve more hours and we'll start to get weekend by thirst and hunger... He knows this.

-But he's getting weaker too.

-It's a game of endurance now, I'm afraid.

-Why doesn't he just get out of that room for a while?

-You may have noticed, there are three exits from the silver room, each leading up to a different part of the house. I have weapons stashed everywhere. If the Warden leaves, even for a minute, he can no longer prevent our escape. We could just lock Ileana in here and get out. I have the only keys.

-He may just gamble if he gets desperate. He does have a one in three chance of picking the right staircase.

-As I said, Urrud doesn't gamble. He'll force the Warden to stay put, for as long as possible.

-Ha! He's fucked.

-Quite right, if we're not fucked first.

-How long can we survive without water, down here?

-Three or four days, I suppose. Only two of them useful, at most.

-Then I think you should tell your spirits to up their game.

-They are doing the best they can.

-Maybe you can tell me a story, while we wait to die... Anything to get my mind off that creature in the corner.

-What would you like to hear?

-That vampire you mentioned seems interesting, maybe even relevant...

-I don't see why not.

-Oh goodie! Thanks, Grandpa Victor!

-Watch it! I'm not that old.

-Ha! Then maybe you should act like it.

-What do you mean?

-All that "dear Madelyn" stuff, as if you're 83, not 43.

-Well...

-Never mind, just tell me about the monstrous vampire.

-As you wish... As it turns out, not all vampires are monsters, but this one was.

-Where did you meet him?

-Northern Italy, in the summer of '98, I think. He owned a large guesthouse in one of the villages, high in the mountains. He even offered a tour where he took tourists to the woods, on lesser-known trials, and showed them spooky things.
-What kind of guests did he usually have?
-Thrill-seekers, usually young people, college students.
-Sounds positively… delicious.
-Ha-ha! If you knew what he did to them, you wouldn't say that.
-Do tell! Can't be any worse than what I've heard so far.
-He had a cave, deep in the mountains, where he would keep his …livestock, often for years. He would come and feed on them occasionally, making sure not to kill them, until…
-Until?
-Until they became sick or reached a certain age, at which point he would just butcher them for meat and feed them to his dogs.
-Sounds like a joyful fella.
-That's not the worst of it. He especially enjoyed the blood of young girls. To procure it, he…
-You know what, I change my mind. I don't need to hear this, especially now. Just skip to the part where you stake the son of a bitch.
-I'm afraid the staking part is just a silly myth. Silver does help, but only in circumstances similar to that room, out there.
-So how did you kill him?
-As usual, I did my homework before approaching him directly. Lorenzo was an old school nobleman, part of an ancient family. He treated what he considered "quality blood", much like we treat good wine. He would store it in freezers, in his cellar, and would only drink it on special occasions. Observing him from the shadows, I realized he

142

placed different bags of blood in different freezers, making sure not to mix them up. I once saw him make a mistake that almost ended him.

-So, the blood could poison him?

-Oh yes. If the person he drank from was even remotely related to him, he would have trouble. That is why he only fed on tourists. When your family is so ancient, practically all the locals are somehow related to you, sharing similar blood.

-What happened to him when he drank that blood?

-Drinking related blood would cause him to temporarily revert to a lesser form, closer to his initial human body.

-So?

-So, if somehow he got two types of blood mixed up, and drank related and unrelated blood at the same time, then that mix would become poisonous. His human body would reject the foreign blood and he would suffer greatly, then die. That is, in fact, how I ended him.

-Couldn't you just chop his head off, or something?

-I could have attempted it, yes, but the old man was... incredibly fast. Besides, I needed to experiment. That knowledge helped me with later vampire hunts.

-Wait! Wait, wait, wait! So, mixing related and unrelated blood did the trick for Lorenzo, right?

-Indeed.

-Are you thinking what I'm thinking?

-Madelyn, the Red Girl isn't... Wait a minute. You may be right.

-I am?

-Yes! Ileana is what I call a "strigoi", not a vampire. But she consumes human and animal flesh as well! That flesh contains blood! Since she seems to be reverting to a more human form, perhaps...

-Perhaps your blood can kill her!

-Keep your voice down. There is a chance, yes. How could I have missed it? Bravo, Madelyn!

-Uhm… Victor?

-What is it?

-It's the Warden. He's approaching the door.

-Get away from there! Close the hatch!

-Done!

-I think it's time we had a little talk with our nemesis.

-Why don't we just… you know.

-Here, take my coat and place it over Ileana. I don't want him to see her current state. We don't need to give him any more information.

-Done.

-Cover her hair well. Give me that syringe, the one that still has a straight needle… Tie this around my arm.

-We should act quickly, in case he makes a move.

-Agreed. Take the syringe and stay where he can't see you. I'm opening the hatch.

-Wait a second!

-What is it?

-Please tell me why this isn't a mistake.

-Because I'm not sure if that syringe in your hand will kill Ileana or… heal her.

-What? We're gambling everything on this?

-Yes.

-What does this have to do with that brute?

-Urrud doesn't gamble.

-You think he knows, don't you?

-Behind this door lies Urrud's Blood Warden.

-Oh… right. But if our mixed blood will kill her, he's not going to tell you. You know that, right?

-I'm counting on it. Stay back and remain silent.

-Ok, ready.

The Red Girl – *Interviews with a monster hunter, by George Hâncu*

CHAPTER 15

A COIN TOSS FOR HUMANITY

-Greetings, my old fired. How is your master doing these days?

-Hello, Victor.

-You don't look so well. I think a bit of fresh air would do you good. Just take any of those doors and don't mind us.

-You don't look too good yourself, hunter.

-I think we're both hunters, Ignacio.

-And assassins... You know, it won't help you.

-What won't?

-Your blood isn't the answer.

-I'm afraid I don't understand.

-I'm going to offer you a deal, Victor.

-Interesting! But I'm not interested.

-Give me the woman, alive, and you may walk out of here unharmed.

-That's not going to happen. It's interesting that you would offer this deal now... Why is that?

-Because you are about to do something foolish, and ruin the Master's prize.

-What prize would that be?

-Playing the fool won't save you, Victor. You will revive the strigoi with that blood, and she will kill you both... The Master can't stop her, not in there.

-Why do you care, Ignacio? That's a win for you, right?

-I need her alive, and I need her now.

-Tough luck, old friend... Oh, I see that scar I left on your right cheek still looks splendid.

-Antagonising me will only make things worse for you, hunter.

-I see your sense of humor hasn't improved much. I guess murdering children will do that to you, right?

-You will regret this, human.

-Human? Look in the mirror, Ignacio. You used to be just like me.

-Weak and pathetic.

-No, my friend. You have never been more weak and pathetic than you are now, but you don't see it. This conversation is over. Good luck out there!

....

-Are you ok, Madelyn? You seem shaken.

-That... thing, his voice pierces into your soul.

-I know. You did great... Here, give me the syringe.

-What do we do now, Victor?

-Urrud's champion just gave us the answer.

-Answer? He offered to spare you if you hand me over to him! Oh, and he told us that our little plan will get us both killed.

-Precisely. He's desperate. He knows my blood could kill the Red Girl.

-That's what you got from the discussion?

-Yes. The Warden's mistake was small but relevant... Think about his proposal.

-I am... It sucks, for us.

-On one hand, he's offering to let us all walk out of here alive: You a captive, Ileana returned to her master, and me a free man.

-Ok...

-On the other hand, he's suggesting that injecting the Red Girl will revive her, getting us both killed.

-Yeah, bad choice.

-He suggests that these are the only options, but they're not. It's a desperate deal.

-Why, for God's sake?

-He makes it sound like he wins, either way, only balancing your life and mine. I get to live while you are doomed, or we both die. This suggests that your capture is more important to Urrud than my life.

-So, I can't be more important than you?

-That doesn't matter if there's a third option, one that he wants us to ignore while we struggle with the choice.

-The option where you inject Ileana and she dies.

-Exactly. In this scenario, his monster dies and we both walk out of here alive. We win everything and he loses everything.

-That sounds too good to be true, Victor.

-I think he doesn't know what happens, if we inject her. I... think it truly is a gamble.

-But Urrud doesn't gamble.

-Exactly, my dear! Urrud doesn't gamble! He needs us to avoid the gamble!

-Fuck! So, if we really want to show the fucker our middle fingers, we force this gamble down his throat.

-It is dangerous, but it is the only option where we stand a chance of ending her and walking out of here.

-Or dying a horrible death.

-I don't know about you, but I'd rather die than hand you over to the Blood Warden. Think about it, if we take this gamble, whatever happens, Urrud doesn't get you.

-Fuck it! Let's do it. At least we'll die with our heads held high.

-I agree, but there's no need to rush. We must use every second at our disposal wisely. Remove the coat, please.

-She's still regressing, Victor.

-Good, that means we have some time.

-Why drag it out?

-To improve our odds, of course. The more time Ignacio spends in that chamber, the weaker he'll get. We should inject her at the last possible moment, when her regression starts to reverse. That way, we may have a chance of escaping, even if the blood wakes her up.

-You're quite the thinker, Victor. I usually go by instinct.

-Your instincts have proven good so far, my dear.

-Yeah, but somehow it all led us to this... coin toss.

-Ha! A coin toss for humanity... I wish it were a coin toss, Madelyn.

-Why?

-Because I don't think our odds are that good.

-Jesus, Victor! What do you think they are?

-One in four, maybe.

-And Urrud still wouldn't accept these odds?

-Not even if it was one in ten, or twenty. He likes to be in control. He likes... choices. He likes forcing hard choices on his victims, choices that usually involve him winning, no matter what.

-Him winning and the victim being corrupted, bit by bit.

-These so-called choices force us towards slowly abandoning our courage and dignity, until we end up just like the monster standing outside that door.

-Yeah, and if that happens, we would be begging for that coin toss.

-But Urrud would never offer it to us... You rest now, my dear. I'll take the next watch.

CHAPTER 16

FREE WILL

-Looks like you're about to fall asleep, Victor.

-Hardly. I'm just trying to conserve the oxygen in here.

-Wait, what?

-It appears that the door, while not being fully airtight, is still blocking most of the air from getting in here.

-Great! So we're about to asphyxiate?

-I don't think so, but we will feel the effects of hypoxia soon.

-Yet another problem we don't need.

-How is our distinguished prisoner doing?

-Still regressing, but I don't know how much longer I can stand this, Victor.

-Don't worry, my dear, it won't be long now.

-How can you tell?

-Besides the fact that her skin and hair are almost human, if it takes much longer, we will be too weak to act. We must carefully balance our growing weakness with Ignacio's, as well as the Red Girl's.

-Seems like we're all slowly dying down here.

-That was the point of this place. I just didn't think we'd be trapped in here with them.

-How much longer, Victor?

-I'd say an hour, at most.

-One hour...

-Yes, I think that will be enough... Ignacio is sitting down. He appears weakened.

-One bloody hour... Victor, are we going to die?

-I'm not going to lie to you, Madelyn, this doesn't look good. I have faced similar odds before, but this time it's different.

-Why is it different?

-This time I may...

-Victor?

-I swore I wouldn't do this again. I swore I wouldn't endanger another innocent... Have I become so reckless?

-It's not your fault, Victor. I was already a target. If anything, your protection kept me alive.

-Yes, until now.

-Victor, I don't blame you. You showed me that this world is more than just piss and dust. I feel strangely grateful, even if I'm about to die... I'm not afraid anymore.

-Well, you should be. If that monster captures you, you will wish for death.

-About that, Victor, if it comes to it, I want you to do it.

-That is very brave of you, Madelyn.

-It's the right thing.

-If it comes to that, I'll try to make it quick.

-Thank you, Victor... Hey, since we may be dead in an hour, can I ask you some personal questions?

-I suppose it doesn't matter now. You can ask me anything.

-Have you... ever been in love?

-Ha!

-What is it?

-Somehow, I knew you were going to ask me that.

-Well, excuse me for the silly girl question!

-I have been in love, once. It was years ago, and it didn't end well.

-What happened?

-I broke my own rule and paid the price. We both did.

-I see...

-What about you, Madelyn? Did you love your husband?

-I... I'm not sure. Maybe. It's all a big blur now.

-Must be the hypoxia setting in.

-That's not funny, Victor.

-I'm sorry.

-How will it happen?

-Madelyn?

-How will you... do it?

-Please, don't concern yourself with that now.

-I want to know. I want to be prepared.

-Madelyn...

-Tell me, Victor!

-All right... We don't have any weapons. Those dammed spears are blunted. I wouldn't have used such a crude instrument on you, anyway... You deserve better.

-How, then?

-I would probably have to... snap your neck with a fast sideways rotation.

-Jesus! Will it hurt?

-I'm not sure... Probably not a lot. It would be quick.

-Ok, ok. Thank you, Victor. I trust you.

-Let's hope it won't come to that.

-You said it yourself: Our odds aren't that good.

-I did say that...

-Well, I guess now would be the best time to ask about what happens when you die. And, as luck would have it, I'm stuck in a death-bunker with a death expert who once died, kind of.

-Well put.

-Do you feel any pain, after?

-None, my dear. As soon as you leave the body, there is no more pain.

-I can't even imagine.

-It's like floating. You don't feel your body anymore. Your senses are sharp, you can move fast and far, without ever tiring.

-That doesn't sound so bad.

-That's only the beginning. Soon, the world begins to fade and a dark veil sets over you... The silence is eerie. If your soul is weak, it will begin to fear.

-But you are still... you? You are still all there?

-For a while, or so I hear. I haven't been that far gone myself.

-What happens after?

-Depending on your life, your memories, and your ties to this world, there are some choices to be made. They aren't obvious choices... They are presented to each spirit differently.

-What choices?

-Well, if you are able to confront your fears and face your own darkness, you may move on to a higher plane.

-And how does one do that?

-That's the real question, isn't it? Most spirits can't, especially the young ones. They are overwhelmed by the weight of the soul, by their own... self-inflicted suffering.

-Self-inflicted? What about the suffering others inflict on them?

-There is only one kind of suffering, Madelyn: The kind we inflict upon ourselves.

-That's just...

-It doesn't make any sense, does it?

-Let's just say it's confusing. I don't need to be confused right now.

-I hope you will understand, one day.

-Not one day, Victor. I need to understand now, since now is all we have. Why is suffering self-inflicted? What about

Urrud? What about his monsters? Do they not inflict themselves upon us?

-It certainly appears so, doesn't it?

-So that's just an illusion?

-They only cause you suffering because you choose to let it happen. From the life you live to all the choices you make, it's all you.

-What about children born in poverty and disease? What choice do they have?

-They made their choice before being born. Suffering is the way we learn, the way we evolve. That's not to say we shouldn't attempt to help those in need, of course.

-What about now, Victor? The Warden is about to hack us to pieces. Isn't that his choice?

-And it is our choice to let him do it, or not.

-Ok, I get that, but it doesn't seem like we always have a choice. Not a real one, anyway.

-But we do, my dear. That is the miracle of free will, of willpower.

-What if it's all predetermined, Victor? What if free will is just an illusion?

-You mean to say that our destinies may be set in stone? Ha-ha-ha!

-What's so funny about that?

-If you only knew what I know, you would realize how ridiculous that statement is.

-Oh, please, enlighten me, Victor. And, if at all possible, don't be condescending.

-I'll try, my dear.

-I appreciate that.

-All right... First of all, let's consider your statement: That it's all just a prewritten story of mathematical precision and singular outcome.

-Ok...

-That world rules out any existential meaning. It also rules out concepts like morality, ethics, and responsibility. Even though it can be argued that it doesn't completely rule out God, it is certainly what atheists seem to think.

-Ok, I get it. If everything is predetermined, then we are all just spectators living with the illusion of free will, being bound to act, live, and die as it was determined, since before we were born.

-Precisely! If that were true, why would we bother to enforce concepts like right and wrong? Why would we think about good and evil, since none of us would have any choice in behaving the way we do? Why would we punish crime? Why would we hold anyone responsible for their actions? It would be like punishing an actor for his character's role in a movie. It's totally absurd!

-Ok, but hold on! I know plenty of atheists who don't act like selfish robots!

-Do you?

-Wait, wait, wait! If atheists truly believed that they have no choice and are not responsible for anything, why isn't this world in flames?

-To begin with, it's because most of them are ignorant. They don't fully comprehend the implications of their ridiculous beliefs. If they did, they would either shoot themselves in the head or, in the case of cowards, they would keep on clinging to their self-proclaimed meaningless and predetermined life, in fear, even though that makes no sense, even to them. That's what I find so ridiculous about these materialistic types, who fundamentally act irrational and against their own beliefs.

-What about all that "make your own meaning" stuff?

155

-How can you make anything of your own, absent free will? Don't you see how illogical that sounds?

-Yeah, you're right, now that I think of it. So, what about the alternative?

-It stands to reason that if you believe in your own freedom to choose, you also believe in a meaningful connection to all things. You believe that your choices impact the world and therefore give you power. You literally become a creator, on your own scale, of course.

-But can't we find a scientific explanation for our freedom to choose?

-Yes and no... Or, not really, if you believe that science rules out God, the way may arrogant idiots who call themselves scientists do, these days.

-Meaning?

-Think about it: If all of us literally create reality for ourselves by observing, choosing, and acting, that means that self-awareness and freedom of choice become fundamental qualities of existence. They, and therefore ourselves, come from beyond this physical world. That is a fact which I have verified, many times.

-But how does this tie to God?

-Again, think about it... Logic is a wonderful thing: If consciousness and freedom of choice are fundamental aspects of reality, then things become simple and beautiful.

-Beautiful?

-Yes! There is literally only one entity that could possess those traits, across all plains of existence. There can only be one fundamental truth, undetermined by any other: The Whole, the never-ending, the all-powerful.

-God...

-If we can truly choose our destiny, then only He could grant this power to us, because only he possesses it.

-So he has made us... like him. Why?

-We cannot know, Madelyn.

-Speculate. If you can't, then who can?

-Maybe it's because He knows himself through us. Maybe He needs to understand limits and death, the only things he can never experience as Himself. Or maybe He just wants us to choose, whatever the choice.

-Maybe He just wants us to choose... to love Him. Maybe He doesn't know if He truly is God.

-Maybe...

-I get it, Victor. For the first time, it's starting to make sense.

-But it can't make sense, Madelyn. Not really. Notice my use of "if". Ultimately, we can never know... Not while inhabiting these bodies.

-But if the "choice" is between a meaningless existence of no self-determination and one of free will, I choose the latter.

-And you shall suffer regardless...

-Why does that have to be, Victor?

-Because you are human. Because you have no guarantees.

-It's not the physical pain that scares me.

-That is wise. Pains of the body must be accepted. True suffering is rooted in the soul and in the mind. Suffering is a conflict form beyond, that can only be conquered if it is first understood.

-How can I do that?

-You can't fully achieve understanding. But belief does offer some comfort... I believe that the fundamental truth of all things is "Coincidentia Oppositorum", a philosophical concept that suggests all contrary things are really the same, and part of the same Whole.

-How does that help with our suffering?

-As I said, suffering implies an unresolved internal conflict. Once you assimilate the idea that all conflicts are illusions, since real conflicts cannot exist, then the problems go away. You just... rise above them.

-Just like that...

-Yes. It is only difficult because of the barriers we have placed ourselves.

-How about you, Victor?

-I still have my share of unexplored darkness, my share of illusions. The body, mind, and soul still torment me, but it feels more like a curable disease than a glooming cancer.

-Why do I sense that this disease can only be cured by death?

-You are correct. But doesn't that mean that death is actually a good thing?

-I suppose so... Well, I guess I'm as ready as I'm ever going to be.

-That is good.

-But I'm still scared, Victor.

-I know. Be brave... It's time.

CHAPTER 17

DEUS EX MACHINA

-How are you doing out there, Ignacio?

-It's all a blur, Victor... You are making the Mater angry.

-Yes, I'm removing the choice from his claws, and forcing a gamble.

-The odds do not favor you. You must know it.

-I do.

-End this foolishness and submit to the Master. His offer will soon expire...

-As will you, by the look of it.

-Time is running out for all of us, Victor.

-Is it really? The only question is, what happens when I decide to open this door?

-You cannot defeat me, Victor.

-Oh, I'm sure... But that's not the point. If your master's prized pet succumbs to my blood, I won't have to.

-You will have to face me, either way.

-No, I won't. If the Red Girl is destroyed, Urrud and his minions will withdraw from our world. That means you too, old friend.

-You are correct. Urrud's minions will withdraw. I, however, no longer count myself amongst them.

-Excuse me?

-The Master... has released me.

-I see... A vengeful act. I must have truly angered him.

-I will hack you to pieces, Victor. Soon...

-You'll try, but if Urrud's energies no longer flow through you, then you are weaker than ever, old friend.
-I'm still more than a match for you, hunter.
-I guess we'll see. Let's continue this discussion some other time. In the meantime, enjoy the view.

....

-Holly crap, Victor! We're fucked!
-I did not expect this move. Urrud has released his champion, just to ensure our untimely demise.
-What are we going to do, Victor? This changes everything.
-It changes nothing. We will do what must be done.
-And we will die, no matter what happens.
-If it must be so, I will not regret it.
-Fuck!
-But now, a new option arises. Ignacio's newfound freedom may work in our favor.
-How? He's clearly still loyal to Urrud... Oh, and he hates your guts.
-That is true. But we can use those things. You see, now we are no longer negotiating with an Elder, but with a fanatical monster.
-And that's somehow better?
-It may be. Ignacio clearly wants to return to Urrud's service. He thinks that will happen once he murders us, in this basement.
-Nice...
-But, If the strigoi is banished, the Army of Shadows will be leaving. Even if Ignacio kills us after, he will have to abandon this body and this world, if he is to re-join his master. Something tells me he's quite fond of both those things.
-So... your pan is what, exactly? To barter with him?

-He knows there is a good chance that he's going to have to leave. His stakes are different than Urrud's, even if he is still loyal.

-You want to create doubt in his mind?

-I want him to think about what happens if we destroy the Red Girl, and Urrud leaves. On top of all those things, what if he is unable to stop us from escaping? He would then have no allies, no protection, and nowhere to run.

-I think he's quite confident in his chances against us.

-I'm not so sure of that... He is weakening fast. There are two of us and we have spears. We could possibly hold him off long enough to escape. Once I get upstairs, things change. The house is filled with weapons that would give us the advantage. I think he knows it.

-That may be, Victor, but he will still go for us.

-He has to... if he believes there is no other choice.

-I'm guessing you have one ready for him?

-I will propose allowing him to leave and live.

-So you will lie to him and hope he doesn't figure it out?

-I will not lie. As long as Ignacio is free from Urrud's influence, he is not a true monster.

-You are not seriously suggesting that this... child-murdering piece of filth deserves a shot at redemption?

-If it were up to me, he would die.

-But it is up to you, Victor! How could you let him go?

-The same way he could let us go. Perhaps it's not my job anymore, to act as judge, jury, and executioner. Perhaps it never was.

-Victor, you are not thinking clearly. It must be that hypoxia thing. Please...

-I'm thinking quite clearly, Madelyn. Urrud would not have anticipated this move... He believes humans to be weak and incapable of change.

-Yeah, and that's true!

-Except for when it isn't. We will prove to him and ourselves that we can step further than ever imagined.

-By bargaining with a murderer and allowing him to walk free? You call that evolved?

-The alternative would be to fight him. I would probably die, and only God knows what would happen to you, my dear. Are you willing to risk that? Are you willing to risk your own soul for a shot at taking him down?

-Yes! Right now I am willing. He doesn't deserve to live.

-I am inclined to agree, but I don't think it's up to us anymore.

-Victor!

-Stay back, I need to talk to him.

....

-Have you considered your choices well, Victor?

-Have you, Ignacio? You are, after all, a free man now.

-I... can never be free.

-Maybe, but maybe not. Only God knows, should you reaffirm your humanity.

-I cannot claim what is no longer mine.

-Believe me, I would love to slit your throat right now, but I decided that it's no longer my choice. Unless you force me to, of course...

-What are you saying, hunter?

-I'm saying that I have decided to roll the dice and inject the strigoi with my blood. That is no longer up for debate. Let's talk about what happens after, shall we?

-You die after.

-If Ileana wakes up, yes, Madelyn and I are done. But what happens if she doesn't wake up? Then, there are two possible outcomes, should you choose to remain stubborn. One: You manage to kill us and then join your former master in worlds beyond, to suffer who knows what horrors and degradations... A hell that I'm sure you deserve, might I ad... Two: We escape upstairs, you follow and die. I got all sorts of fun surprises waiting for you up there. Who knows what will happen to your tormented soul then? Not even Urrud will take you back if you fail...

-I'll take my chances.

-Why risk it? There are two of us and we have spears. Your sword is at a disadvantage.

-You overestimate yourselves.

-Maybe... But there's another option. One that doesn't involve a fight to the death.

-I will not make a deal with you, Victor.

-Even it means saving your soul?

-There is nothing to save.

-Oh, but I think there might be. Again, don't get me wrong. There is nothing I would enjoy more than seeing you take your last breaths in agony.

-Speak, then.

-Walk out of here and never return. If the Red Girl dies and you walk away, your life is once again your own. I will not pursue you.

-You think I'm scared of you, hunter?

-You would be a fool not to be scared of me, Ignacio. Your strength will not save you from an arrow in the neck.

-This discussion is pointless. Urrud's strigoi will tear you to pieces. Your version of events will never take place. Not in this world.

-But what if it does?

-You are mad!

-What if, Ignacio?

-If luck favors you, we will talk again. I won't insult Urrud by betraying him.

-You mean betraying him before you know.
-We shall see... Go ahead, inject the strigoi.

....

-Here, Victor. You should do it.
-Thank you.
-Remember... remember what we talked about. I don't want pain.
-I am proud of you, Madelyn. You are proving Urrud wrong with every breath.
-I hope you're right, Victor.
-Hold on...
-What is it?
-I need to stop. He... He is here.
-Who? Who's here, Victor?
-The Messenger is... here.
-Who? Wait... the Messenger from the pond, from when you were a kid?
-Yes...
-You're joking.
-I'm afraid not.
-What does this mean, Victor?
-I'm not quite sure... This...this has never happened before.
-Didn't you ever speak to him, after that night?
-He... said he would return. He said that we would speak again, but we never did.
-It seems like that's about to change.
-This is big, Madelyn.
-I know. That guy literally made you what you are.
-That's not the point.
-What is it, then?
-You see, the Messenger is Hermes himself. I discovered that much later.

-Hermes? As in… the Greek god Hermes?

-Hermes, Thoth, Mercury… whatever you want to call him.

-An actual god?

-An Elder… One much more powerful than Urrud or Sassom.

-But that's good, isn't it?

-I don't know… Madelyn, please move to that corner.

-Wh…Why?

-There will be a bright flash of light. Don't be scared. Just sit down and cover your eyes.

-What about you?

-I will enter a trance-like state. We'll talk once it has passed.

-How long will that take? Don't leave me here alone!

-Don't worry, my dear. No shadow may linger in his presence.

-Wait, Victor!

…………………………………………………………………………………………………..

-Great Hermes, I am honored.

-I great you, child.

-I am in desperate need of your council, Elder One.

-I may offer you some council.

-I need help, wise Hermes.

-I have come to release you from my service.

-I do not understand.

-You may renounce your mission. You need not be a hunter any longer.

-Wh..why? Why now?

-Your burden has become too heavy, child.

-But I have not completed my mission, wise Hermes.

-You have, Victor. This point in time is as far as I could ask a human to go. You and your companion are willing to die, in the service of humanity.

-We are. We accept that.

-You need not do it, young one.

-I have never given up on my tasks!

-I know. It is time to rest, child.

-Rest... How can I rest? What will become of the Red Girl? What will become of humanity?

-That is not for you to determine.

-I understand that my action is a gamble.

-A gamble the outcome of which no observer can predict, not even in the Higher Realms. Your blood is entangled with Ileana's and Madelyn's, more than you know.

-Entangled?

-You are related to them, child. Distant, but still dangerous. The wave may collapse on either side.

-I see...

-Ileana's blood is conquered by darkness, and Madelyn's is infused with light. Combined, they have placed the strigoi into a state of uneasy slumber.

-And my blood?

-You are a mixture of both light and darkness, Victor, in near-perfect balance.

-Have I not proven myself, wise Hermes?

-You have proven many things, child. You need not prove any more.

-Will you not allow me the chance to save humanity from Urrud's scourge?

-I will not stop you, Victor... But understand this: Your actions may also damn humanity, not rescue it from corruption.

-What is there to be done, Elder One? The monster will soon wake! Will you not smite it?

-I will not interfere in such a manner.

-Then you have truly damned us, Hermes.

-Remember, Victor, we must not surrender ourselves to chaos, no matter the cost. You can choose to fight the darkness or the light, but if you abandon your fate to chance, you renounce your gift… You renounce Him and become Her herald.

-I understand.

-It is not you that I worry about. It is your companion. Her soul can become a vessel of chaos, Her vessel.

-Urrud's plan was… brilliant. I never expected it.

-His knowledge is vast, but he has masters of his own.

-None that would desire to summon the Dark Mother, surely.

-Such things are beyond you, young one.

-He wanted me to do what he never would. He… wanted me to take the chance. I was wrong.

-That is why I'm here, Victor. Unlike Urrud's masters, I believe in humanity. I must.

-I do not understand.

-Because you have yet to stand in the Creator's presence. You and I are more alike than you think, child.

- I am humbled by your words, Elder One.

-Your chosen mission has ended, Victor. Please, reconsider your choices.

-I need to know more…

-I must leave you now. My presence here was intrusive enough. We shall speak again when you have shed this skin.

…………………………………………………………………………………………………

-Victor! Are you ok?

-I'm awake. How long was I out?

-Out? You just finished your sentence and dropped to the floor.

-Interesting.

-Well? What happened?

-Hermes asked me to reconsider my choices.

-Meaning?

-It appears that me injecting the Red Girl was all part of Urrud's plan.

-I thought he didn't like gambles. I thought he didn't lie and cheat. What changed?

-He doesn't take gambles and he didn't lie.

-Oh, I see... He allowed his newly freed pet to do it. Brilliant!

-As for taking a chance, it appears that was not his choice to make. He answers to a higher Elder.

-What did he hope to achieve?

-Urrud's master needs to meet the Dark Mother. For what purpose, I cannot know.

-I remember Her... You told me about Her in that faceless monk story. She seems like... pure evil.

-Not evil. Chaos, or, even worse, nothingness.

-She sounded like the Anti-God. I could never have imagined something so sinister.

-I don't even know who or what She is, but I know it's big, bigger than perhaps any Elder.

-Bigger than Hermes himself?

-Perhaps bigger than our Creator, my dear.

-The Creator? Oh... I keep forgetting that He's not God.

-He's just a part of God, as are we all.

-As is the Dark Mother?

-Strangely enough, yes. It must be so.

-I will never understand this, Victor.

-You don't need to. You already understand more than most humans. Be thankful for what you have.

-It's hard to be thankful when I feel like every minute may be my last.

-Well, you need not feel that about this particular minute.

-That's a relief. Do we have a new plan, then?

-Not yet.

-Fuck!

-Have patience, Madelyn. We must consider our options carefully.

-Well, if I understand things correctly, we may no longer inject Ileana with your blood.

-That would be ill-advised, yes.

-But she's going to recover eventually, Victor.

-True. Adding to the problem, we have no guaranteed means of destroying her at our disposal.

-You made that pretty clear.

-All we can do is damage and pacify her, for a while.

-So, can we restrain her indefinitely?

-Not likely, especially with Urrud's army constantly knocking at our front door.

-That is what he wanted, right? To pressure you into taking the desperate gamble, to make you feel like there was no other way.

-It seems that his masters have bigger plans for this world than just unleashing Urrud's corruption upon it. We must take that into account.

-Doesn't it mean that the Red Girl was just a pawn all along, whose role was to bait you into unwillingly summoning the Dark Mother?

-That's obvious, yes.

-But wait, that means that she's not so important, after all. Maybe you just chose to make her important, by accepting Urrud's twisted game.

-That is also obvious, yes.

-And since we're stating the obvious, doesn't that mean that we don't really have to concern ourselves with her anymore? I mean, fuck her! Let her rot in here or just set her free... Whatever.

-Interesting...

-What is?

-I can't believe that Urrud would base his entire plan on my willingness to inject the strigoi with my blood.

-He needs you to do it willingly, right?

-Yes, he needs me to use free will and abandon humanity's fate to chaos, to chance.

-Fuck!

-What is it, Madelyn?

-What if...

-Yes?

-What if he doesn't necessarily need... you to do it?

-...Ignacio.

-Fucking Ignacio!

-He's reverting to human form. He's regaining free will and is fully aware of this choice.

-Shit, Victor! What if he overpowers you and then uses your blood on Ileana?

-Then, Urrud wins.

-Either way, the fucker wins!

-I told you, that's what he does. If Ignacio manages to inject Ileana, his Army of Shadows may or may not leave, but the Dark Mother still comes.

-Then the choice is simple, Victor: It's either him or us... all of us.

-It would seem so... But we have one more problem.

-And that is?

-You see, there is another who can choose to inject the Red Girl.

-M... Me? You must be joking!

-You are also aware of the choice and are able to make it.

-I would never do it, Victor!

-Even to save me from Ignacio?

-I... even so, yes. Give me that syringe! I'll destroy it myself!

-Here you go.

-There! Crushed to pieces!

-But there are more of them upstairs. You know where they are, Madelyn...

-Victor! I would never do it! You need to trust me.

-I... cannot. It is also a gamble.

-Victor?

-It's essentially the same gamble. Damn it!

-No it's not, Victor! Look at me! It can't be! ...Besides, we can defeat him, right?

-I do not know. It is all entangled... every choice.

-What does your gut tell you?

-Damn it! My gut tells me that Ignacio is weaker than he has ever been. My gut tells me to go for it, before Ileana wakes up and hacks the three of us to small, bloody pieces.

-Ha! Perhaps that would be better. Then there would be no one left to inject her.

-No one, for now, but Urrud may find another, of similar blood. That is if Ignacio doesn't somehow escape.

-Shit! What do we do?

-I can only see one favorable outcome: We go out there now, while we still have our strength, we disable or kill Ignacio and we keep the Red Girl locked up.

-For a second there, I thought you were going to kill me...

-Despite the considerable pain that would cause me, I have briefly considered it.

-Fuck you, Victor!

-Ha-ha! Besides, if I kill you now, I would have to face Ignacio alone. But, like the old saying goes: Two blunt wooden spears are better than one!

-How do I use this thing properly?

-Keep both hands on it. One in the middle and one towards the back.

-Ok...

-Always keep it pointing at him. Never hesitate, not even for a second. When you thrust, do it quickly and put as much weight into it as possible. Like this... Go for the body and head. Then, quickly return to a defensive position and wait for his attacks.

-Fuck!

-He will try to cut the spears with his sword. Try to pull back when he does that, then hit hard and fast. Use all your strength.

-Don't know how much strength I have left.

-Enough to throw him off balance with a good hit. I'll do the rest. When you have a chance, run towards the second exit, on the right. It leads to the armory.

-Got it.

-I keep a few loaded crossbows there, in the display chase. Grab one as fast as you can then. Find the trigger. It works just like a gun: Just point and shoot.

-Believe it or not, I have actually shot a crossbow before.

-Really?

-It was years ago, but I still remember how it works.

-We are in luck, then. One good shot will disable Ignacio.

-All right. Just make sure to get out of the way, please.

-I will try to, but if the need arises, take the shot regardless. Do not hesitate.

-You keep saying that.

-Ignacio is a killer, Madelyn. One wrong move and we're done. Do you understand that?

-I do...Victor, Ileana is starting to turn dark.

-I've noticed. We are out of time, I'm afraid.

-I'm right behind you. Go!

CHAPTER 18

IGNACIO

-Hello again, Victor. I understand you had a visitor.

-I'm going to open this door now, Ignacio.

-Then you are a fool.

-You can still choose to leave.

-I'm afraid I'm not going anywhere, Victor... But you know that.

-We shall see...

-You have decided not to inject the strigoi. Perhaps you are a coward after all.

-The time for talking is done. When I unlock the door, you are free to make your move. We will make ours.

-Go ahead, Victor.

....

-Ok, Madelyn, the door opens towards Ignacio. He knows it but has not moved out of the way.

-What does that mean?

-It means that he has no intention of letting us get out of this room. The mirror room is larger and gives us the advantage.

-He's afraid?

-He's smart. He wants to wait us out. If we die in here before he goes insane out there, then he can find a way to open the door and use my blood.

-If Ileana doesn't butcher him as she will us!

-Yes. Maybe he still believes he can get us to inject her.

-Regardless, we have to fight our way out of here.
-Yes. Ready?
-Ready!
-Ok…The door is unlocked.
-He's not coming in.
-I was right. We have to push the door open.
-Fuck. He's heavier than we are combined, Victor.
-Push, Madelyn!
-We're hitting him!
-He's pushing back! Harder!
-I'm pushing as hard as I can!
-Don't drop your spear! Be ready!
-We can't get out, Victor!
-Let it close! Step back!
-Ok, what now?
-He's forcing us to go out one by one, while he's pushing on the door. He will cut us down if we try that.
-What now?
-Close the hatch and be silent.
-Ok.
-Shhhh! Move towards the back of the room, quietly.
-On three?
-Look at my fingers…
-Ahhh!
-Go, go, go!
-He's down, hit him!
-Keep your spear up, Madelyn!
-I hit him!
-Run! Second door! There!
-Hold on, Victor! I'll be back!

……………………………………………………………………………………………………

-You're bleeding, Ignacio. It seems that your master has truly abandoned you.

-Yes... But you're not going anywhere, Victor. Turn your back on me and I'll cut you down.

-What's stopping you from cutting me down now?

-Nothing. I just need your foolish little sidekick to return.

-Why?

-She needs to witness what happens to those who defy the Master.

-Are you sure you don't need her for something else?

-The time for games has ended, Victor!

-Now, Madelyn!

....

-Ha! Got you, motherfucker!

-Ahhh!

-Victor! What the fuck happened?

-The bolt went right through him, and into me.

-Shit! I don't know that could happen.

-These things are more powerful than you think.

-Well, I got him in the chest and you in the shoulder. Could have been worse!

-Ahh! Can't... argue with that...

-We did it. Victor! He's gone!

-He's not dead. Hurry!

-What are we doing?

-Drag him in there, with Ileana!

-He's not going anywhere, Victor.

-We have seconds left! Urrud has reclaimed his body!

-Fuck! He's moving!

-Push him in there!

-He won't let go, Victor! He's crushing my arm!

-I can't release you! Urrud has given him all his strength back!
-He's getting up, Victor! Use his sword!
-If I touch that sword, we're both dead!
-Then go! Lock us both in here before it's too late! Now!
-Madelyn!
-Close the door, in the name of humanity!
-Damn it! Damn it to hell!
-Lock it, quickly! I can't hold him back.
-It's… done. I'm so sorry, my dear.
-It's ok, Victor. We stopped him! He can't do anything now.
-…Madelyn, where is the bolt?
-The arrow?
-Step away from him Madelyn! Don't say a word!

....

-Here's your bolt, hunter… Hmmm, I can smell your blood.
-Welcome back, Ignacio… That hole in your heart must really hurt.
-It does not matter. The Master is keeping me alive.
-Not for long. His influence will fade in there, just like with the strigoi. You are dead, Ignacio.
-I have been dead for a long time.
-Leave Madelyn be. She's of no further use to you.
-Just open the door and I'll allow her to walk out.
-Don't open the door, Victor!
-Be quiet, Madelyn!
-I think your friend and I will get to know each other a lot better.
-Don't you dare, you beast!
-I think it's time we had some fun. Don't you, Madelyn?
-Don't touch me!
-Madelyn, listen to me carefully…

-Go ahead, Victor!

-Don't do it, whatever happens, don't do it!

-Do what, Victor?

-Don't kill yourself.

-I... understand.

-Enough! Be silent, hunter!

-Fuck you, Ignacio! Madelyn, he wants you to stab Ileana with that bolt. Do you understand?

-I understand.

-Silence, woman!

-Ahhh! He's breaking my arm, Victor!

-You piece of shit!

-No more games! You will pierce the strigoi's skin with this bolt, woman... If you do not, I will break every bone in your body, one by one.

-I thought you needed me to do this willingly. I thought you needed me to choose.

-Listen to me, my dear. You do have a choice. Think carefully.

-Silence!

-I get it, Victor.

-Take the bolt and stab the strigoi! Do it now!

-Take the bolt, Madelyn!

-I'm sorry, Victor!

-Madelyn!

-Foolish woman!

-Good... bye, Victor. Let them... rot... in here.

-She is... gone. You have lost, Ignacio. Soon, you will join her.

-Yes... I can feel the Master's strength leaving my body. Your prison works well, hunter.

-Good! I hope Ileana wakes up before you die, so she can tear you to pieces.

-I wish you could do it instead, hunter. It would be a more fitting end.

-You don't deserve an execution, you abomination!

-We both know you want to do it, Victor. Perhaps you have a chance if you are fast enough.

-And we both know that as soon as I open that door, Urrud's vile influence will restore you.

-Well then, are you going to watch me die, Victor?

-Gladly.

-You know, I think you were right.

-Shut up and die!

-I did have a chance to save my soul, but I wasted it.

-No, you didn't. You never deserved one. You deserve to die.

-The strigoi awakens soon.

-I'll enjoy this.

-It's funny, Victor.

-What is?

-Did you know that a person can still function without a beating heart, for a few seconds?

-Just accept your fate, Ignacio.

-This bolt… It's now drenched in all our blood. I suppose it would be a fitting tool for ending humanity. Don't you think so?

-It won't work, Ignacio. As soon as Urrud leaves you completely, you will drop dead.

-We… shall see.

-You motherfucker!

-You seem… worried… Victor. Perhaps you… need to come in here and… finish me yourself, before it's… too late.

-I'm not that stupid, Ignacio. Besides, you need to ask yourself one question: How do you want to spend your last moments as a human being? Condemning us to destruction or gathering what little dignity you have left and dying like a man?

-I have made my choice, Hunter. Make yours.

-Fuck you, Ignacio! Do it! Stab her! While you still have the strength!

-Not yet… old friend. Not yet…

-Remember who you are, Ignacio!

-I am a piece of filth… Victor. You said it… yourself. The funny thing is, you and I are not so different…

-That's bullshit, and you know it! Just die!

-Soon… I am… becoming fully human. I can feel it.

-Put that bolt down, Ignacio. If you are like me, then you won't do it.

-That's… where you are wrong, old… friend. That's exactly why I'm going to… do it.

-No! No, no, no!

-It's… done. You can open the… door now, Victor. I won't allow Urrud to retake me. He won't tolerate… this betrayal.

-Betrayal? …Ignacio? Fuck!

-Your nemesis… dies today.

-Fuck! Key, key, key! …Madelyn! …Thank God! You're still alive!

CHAPTER 19

TO BE HUMAN

-Hey! Relax! You're ok! You're safe!

-Victor? Where am I?

-In bed… still in my house, still alive. Maria has been taking care of you.

-Shit! My neck hurts like hell.

-That's what happens when you stab yourself with a crossbow bolt. Luckily, you narrowly missed your jugular.

-Lucky me… What happened, Victor?

-After you tried to nobly off yourself, Ignacio decided to have a go at the Red Girl, himself.

-Wait… didn't he have to be like us, to do that.

-He did and… he was, in the end.

-So, we're doomed, I guess. The Dark Mother will soon erase us from existence.

-I'm not so sure about that.

-What do you mean? What happened?

-The bolt actually killed Ileana.

-For good? Like, for real?

-For real.

-So… your blood did the trick. Fantastic!

-Our blood did the trick.

-Yours and mine? That's right! That damned arrow was stained with my blood as well.

-Remember, Ileana already had your blood inside her.

-Wait, you mean…

-I think it was Ignacio's blood. The bolt sliced through his heart... Nice shot, by the way.

-Thank you. So, his blood was the missing ingredient?

- It was quite obvious, really... I don't know why it didn't occur to me.

-Slow down. How?

-You see, Ignacio was Urrud's Blood Warden, and for good reason. His blood had power over all the monsters.

-I don't get it.

-He started out pure, as a man of God. Corrupting Ignacio was Urrud's greatest triumph. Before, his blood could slay any monster. After the corruption was completed, it was quite the opposite: The Warden's blood would heal his master's countless minions...

-Coincidentia Oppositorum! Ha!

-Exactly, my dear. As Ignacio once again turned human, his blood somehow... remembered. Suddenly, pure darkness became pure light.

-Unbelievable. That damned arrow went through his heart after Urrud released him! Ha-ha! Victor, this is unbelievable luck!

-I don't think so, my dear. I think Ignacio knew what he was doing.

-From the start?

-I think his long stay in my mirror room somehow... did the trick. It reminded him of what he once stood for. I think he meant for this to happen.

-I was curious why you were still alive when I returned with the crossbow. I half expected you to be dead.

-Ignacio waited for you to return. He said as much... I think he somehow managed to deceive Urrud himself.

-Unbelievable.... That fucking murderer? How? Why?

-I'm not sure, my dear, but it haunts me...

-What does?

-Something he said... Two things actually: He said that he and I were not so different.

-Funny.

-That's what he said too, that it was funny.

-And the second thing?

-He said: "Your nemesis dies today".

-The Red Girl, yes.

-I'm not so sure he was talking about her.

-Who then? Himself?

-Not so sure about that either.

-I see... So, we're safe, then?

-Not at all.

-Why did I know you were going to say that?

-Ha-ha! Your instincts once again reveal the truth!

-Well, at least you did your job, Victor. You didn't gamble with the fate of humanity, you foiled Urrud's plan and you killed two of his most powerful monsters.

-We killed them... and Ignacio kind of helped.

-Hmmm... Do you really think that monster could really redeem himself, just like that?

-I don't know, my dear. But it does make me wonder...

-Decades of atrocities, followed by one choice, to just... wash everything away?

-One very important choice. But I don't think it washed anything away.

-Nothing can wash that away.

-Perhaps that's what it means to be human, my dear. To constantly move through darkness and light, as if stepping on the tiles of a chessboard... Light, then darkness... then light again and so on. Until we die.

-Yeah, but it seems like not all tiles are equal, does it.

-Perhaps. Food for taught.

-So, since you didn't kill the Red Girl yourself, I'm guessing that Urrud is still out there, preparing his revenge.

-Quite right. And I'm afraid he's more determined than usual.

-We have to defend ourselves, Victor.

-It's not just us who are under attack.

-I know, it's all of us. We have to fight for everything human.

-We have to fight to stay human, my dear.

-Ha! Humans fighting to remain human.

-I guess that's also part of what it means to be... human.

-I guess so.

-You rest now. We will talk again once you have regained your strength.

CHAPTER 20

PAST, PRESENT, AND FUTURE

-Hello, Victor.

-Who are you? This is private property!

-Oh, I'm just a gardener, looking for a job.

-How did you know my name, then?

-You were recommended.

-I see... I don't need a gardener right now. Thank you.

-Well, it looks like your home and indeed your back yard need some work. It is a big property, after all.

-Look, I'm busy. Please leave.

-I'll tell you what, I'll work for free, the first day. That way you can judge my merit, with no strings attached.

-Who are you, really? I don't have time for games!

-You have all the time you need, Victor.

-Answer my question or get out!

-I already did, son.

-You are testing my patience, old man.

-Look, just go about your business. I'll get to work on those flowers... We'll talk again later.

-Jesus! You don't give up, do you?

-A father never gives up on his son, Victor.

-Wh... What did you say?

-I'm so sorry, my boy. You... live a lonely life. It needn't be so.

-What did you say? What is your name? ...Answer me!

-You know my name, Victor... You were so young but you remember everything, don't you?

-Fa....Father? Dad? It can't be. This is a joke!

-My son, you have many gifts. Don't deny the answers that are screaming at you. You felt who I was, from the moment you set eyes upon me. But you don't know everything... No one does.

-Why? Why... now? Why after all these years? Damn you!

-Because you need me. Why did you run from me, Victor?

-I... was just a boy... a scared little boy.

-You were exceptional. You never gave up on life but you did give up on me.

-I didn't know... I followed my instincts.

-Come here, my son.

-Dad!... Oh, God! I'm sorry!

-You needn't feel sorry, Victor. Look at all the things you have achieved... I am proud of you.

-Dad...

-You have a brother... Did you know that? His name is Vlad.

-Brother? No, I didn't know.

-He's ten years younger than you, and a fool! Ha! Just as stubborn as you are.

-Where do you think we got that from?

-Ha-ha! Good point, my boy!

-Can I meet him? Although, now really isn't a good time.

-I know you have many troubles, Victor. But it's always a good time to learn something new, don't you think?

-Are you going to lecture me about my life now? I guess you have more than three decades of lectures to catch up on.

-I'm not going to lecture you... Although, the way you've been treating those poor rose bushes, it would seem like you need a good talking to!

-Ha-ha! Maria doesn't know how to do it properly. I guess I need a real gardener.

-We all do, son, whatever the nature of our chosen garden.

-Wait, weren't you a doctor? How did you get so... mystical?

-You learn many things when you consider time your friend, not your enemy.

-Well, I've always felt like my life was a race against time. That's not to say I didn't get my fair share of lessons, along the way.

-Yes... many lessons. The lessons, they never stop coming, no matter how old you get. Did you know that?

-I suspected as much... Dad, how was your life? Were you happy? Did I make you suffer?

-I was and I am happy. But I did also suffer. Such is the curse of all beings bearing a particular identity, no matter how vast.

-I guess so...

-I sometimes wish I could return to being just a child, like you, Victor.

-I'm hardly a child anymore, dad.

-...You know, when I made all of this, I never intended it to be so messy, so complicated. That was perhaps the mistake of my own youth.

-Dad? What is this?

-I'm sorry, Victor. I shouldn't burden you with such things.

-Dad, I feel strange... What's happening? The spirits have gone silent.

-Yes... they get scared whenever I reveal myself. I can't say I blame them.

-I've never felt anything like this before.... Urrud, Sassom, I don't feel their presence anymore. What are you?

-I'm sure that Balthazar's minions could use a break. After all, they have been working restlessly.

-Who is Balthazar? Who are you?

-I'm your father, Victor.

-Are you really?

-Amongst many other things, yes.

-I've never... felt such power. Not even Hermes...

-Your brother is worried about you. As am I.

-Vlad?

-Him, not so much. He has yet to learn of your existence.

-You mean... Can it really be You, Father?

-I am here, Victor.

-I am humbled... I don't understand... I feel so useless.

-You don't need to feel humbled by me, Victor. And you are anything but useless.

-How may I be of service? Please tell me, my Lord.

-You're doing a pretty good job so far, Victor. I did promise not to lecture you, remember?

-But I have so many questions.

-And there will be a time for answers. There always is. Past, present, and future, they are all aspects of Him, Victor.

-Have you... stood in His presence, my Lord?

-We all do, Victor. You do too, every second of every day. But you already know that, don't you?

-What am I to do?

-Whatever you desire, my son. There is just one thing that I would ask of you. Your younger brother will need your guidance, in the days ahead. Will you aid him along his own road?

-I will do my best, my Lord.

-Excellent! I am in your debt.

-How will I find him?

-That won't be a problem for you, Victor.

-I understand.

-You go now, please. Take care of the innocent who has sacrificed much for us. I shall see about those roses of yours.

-My Lord...

-Call me Herumai.

-I dare not.

-It is the name given to me, by my own Father. It was in another time and space, but some things transcend even those boundaries.

-Your own Father?

-Yes... an ambitious Creature! I... also parted from Him, when I was very young. I remember how scared I felt, believing I was all alone. It wasn't a forest but a vast, dark space. The feeling, however, is quite similar.

-I would ask you about your Mother.

-I will tell you all about Her, sometime. Or perhaps someone else will.

-I am grateful, Father.

-As am I, Victor... As am I.

CHILDREN OF HERUMAI SERIES
-END OF PART I-

BY GEORGE HÂNCU

Printed in Great Britain
by Amazon

75730042R00108

NO
FRIEND
TO
THIS
HOUSE

NATALIE HAYNES

NO FRIEND TO THIS HOUSE

MANTLE

First published 2025 by Mantle
an imprint of Pan Macmillan
The Smithson, 6 Briset Street, London EC1M 5NR
EU representative: Macmillan Publishers Ireland Ltd, 1st Floor,
The Liffey Trust Centre, 117–126 Sheriff Street Upper,
Dublin 1 D01 YC43
Associated companies throughout the world
www.panmacmillan.com

ISBN 978-1-5290-6154-3 HB
ISBN 978-1-5290-6155-0 TPB

3 5 7 9 8 6 4 2

A CIP catalogue record for this book is available from the British Library.

Illustrations and map by Hemesh Alles

Typeset by Palimpsest Book Production Ltd, Falkirk, Stirlingshire
Printed and bound in the UK using 100% Renewable Electricity by
CPI Group (UK) Ltd

Visit www.panmacmillan.com to read more about all our books
and to buy them.

To Maria, with love